HIGH HURDLES

Close
Quarters

Books by Lauraine Snelling

RED RIVER OF THE NORTH

An Untamed Land
A New Day Rising
A Land to Call Home
The Reaper's Song

HIGH HURDLES

Olympic Dreams	*Out of the Blue*
DJ's Challenge	*Storm Clouds*
Setting the Pace	*Close Quarters*

GOLDEN FILLY SERIES

The Race	*Shadow Over San Mateo*
Eagle's Wings	*Out of the Mist*
Go for the Glory	*Second Wind*
Kentucky Dreamer	*Close Call*
Call for Courage	*The Winner's Circle*

HIGH HURDLES

Close Quarters

LAURAINE SNELLING

BETHANY HOUSE PUBLISHERS
MINNEAPOLIS, MINNESOTA 55438

Published by Bethany House Publishers
A Ministry of Bethany Fellowship International
11300 Hampshire Avenue South
Minneapolis, Minnesota 55438

Printed in the United States of America by
Bethany Press International, Minneapolis, Minnesota 55438

Library of Congress Cataloging-in-Publication Data

Snelling, Lauraine.
    Close quarters / by Lauraine Snelling.
        p.   cm. — (High hurdles ; 6)
    Summary: DJ prays for guidance as she tries to balance her
time at the riding academy with school work, art projects, and her
new stepfamily.
    ISBN 0-7642-2034-9 (pbk.)
    [1. Horses—Fiction. 2. Stepfamilies—Fiction. 3. Christian
life—Fiction.] I. Title. II. Series: Snelling, Lauraine. High
hurdles ; bk. 6.
PZ7.S677Co   1997
[Fic]—dc21   97-33859
                                                           CIP
                                                            AC

To every reader who says
reading HIGH HURDLES
and GOLDEN FILLY books
has changed her life.
Thank you, Heavenly Father.

LAURAINE SNELLING fell in love with horses by age five and never outgrew it. Her first pony, Polly, deserves a book of her own. Then there was Silver, Kit—who could easily have won the award for being the most ornery horse alive—a filly named Lisa, and an asthmatic registered Quarter Horse called Rowdy, and Cimeron, who belonged to Lauraine's daughter, Marie. It is Cimeron who stars in *Tragedy on the Toutle*, Lauraine's first horse novel. All of the horses were characters, and all have joined the legions of horses who now live only in memory.

While there are no horses in Lauraine's life at the moment, she finds horses to hug in her research, and she dreams, like many of you, of owning one or three again. Perhaps a Percheron, a Peruvian Paso, a . . . well, you get the picture.

Lauraine lives in California with her husband, Wayne, basset hound Woofer, and cockatiel Bidley. Her two sons are grown and have dogs of their own; Lauraine and Wayne often dogsit for their golden retriever granddogs. Besides writing, reading is one of her favorite pastimes.

1

DJ RANDALL COULDN'T BELIEVE her eyes—or ears.

"I wanna go with DJ!" Bobby Crowder screamed. Or was it Billy? It didn't matter. Tears strained down the five-year-old twins' matching red faces. Between flailing feet and arms, they were lucky someone didn't get hurt. Especially them. And to think these two were now DJ's brothers. Scary thought.

"Don't *wanna* go with Nanny Ria!" The second outdid the first in lung power.

Maria Ramos, the nanny who'd been caring for the twins since their mother had died three years earlier, looked about ready to cry, too—or yell. Neither action was quite appropriate in front of the club where they had just held the wedding reception for DJ's mother, Lindy, and Robert, the twins' father. The new Mr. and Mrs. Robert Crowder charged out of the club's open doors when the shouts reached the decibel level of a marching band.

"What is going on here?" Robert laid a hand on each boy's shoulder. He had to squeeze some to get their attention.

DJ watched the squirming twins from the sidelines. She never had been one to volunteer for bruised shins. Unless, of course, she got them working with a horse. Then it didn't matter.

Besides, in the long mauve dress and matching satin shoes she'd worn for the wedding, she doubted she could leap fast enough to keep up with the furious five-year-olds. Let alone calm them down. Her mouth dropped open. Her mother, Mrs. Perfectly Groomed, was kneeling on the concrete in her long, full ivory dress to comfort one of the hiccuping boys. When she stood up, the dress wore black knee prints, but Lindy didn't even notice.

Gran and Joe joined the scene. By now the twins had quit crying, but their lower lips quivered like fresh Jell-O Jigglers. Robert picked up the boys, and they buried their faces in the collar of his black tuxedo as Lindy stroked the back of the nearest one and murmured to them both.

DJ paused to examine the weird feeling that now wriggled its way to her attention. Like there was plate glass between the rest of the family and her. Like she was looking from the outside in. *This is stupid*, she told herself. *Get over there and . . . and what? Play big sister? That's what you are now, so get on it*.

"We wants DJ." The boys pulled their we-think-talk-and-act-the-same trick that always amazed her. Just because they were identical twins, did they have some invisible connection?

Like a swimmer coming up for air, DJ broke out of her fog and crossed the sidewalk. She ordered her mouth to smile, putting the weird stuff out of her mind. She tried to kill the feeling of being an outsider but only succeeded in burying it.

"Hey, guys, what's up?"

Smiles peeked out from beneath the tear streaks. "Don't want to go to our house with Nanny Ria."

"Want to go to Grandpa's house with you." Identical sniffs as two pudgy hands wiped under two snub noses.

"Gross, you two. Get a tissue." She stepped back, but her grin said she was teasing. It worked. The smiles came out. Even with the Double Bs smiling, DJ was grateful the twins were on their way back to Robert's old San Francisco house to stay with their nanny. She had been dreaming of a whole week with Gran and GJ—Grandpa Joe—alone.

One boy coughed, then the other.

Gran put a hand on each forehead. She looked up at Robert.

"Trouble, huh?" he asked.

Gran nodded, her silver-shot gold hair ruffling in the breeze. "No wonder they're being so fussy."

"Okay, fellas, how about your mommy and I take you back home and get you settled?" Robert eyed the boys with concern.

"DJ too?"

"No, not DJ. She has to go to school on Monday, and she can't drive herself, remember?"

"Grandpa could come get her."

Gran ruffled the talker's hair. "You have all the answers, don't you?" She put an arm around DJ's waist. "DJ has to help me put all the stuff away so you have a home to come to next week. I need her more than you do." She raised on tiptoe and kissed each boy's hot cheek. "I bet Nanny Ria has Popsicles in the freezer for you when you get home."

The Double Bs looked at each other and then lay their heads back on their father's shoulders. They really didn't look like they felt very good. DJ patted their backs. "You guys be good, okay?"

They nodded.

Robert's younger brother, Andy, drove up with Robert's Bronco, and Robert belted the boys into the rear seat, motioning for Maria to get in on the other side. When the twins started to whimper again, Robert and Lindy waved to everyone, and Robert helped her tuck her wedding dress around her feet so it wouldn't get caught in the door. With another wave, they drove off, leaving DJ feeling lost, like a little kid trapped in a pitch-black room. Her mother had been so concerned about the boys, she hadn't even hugged her daughter. And they'd be gone on their honeymoon for more than a week.

DJ shrugged. "Oh well," she whispered. But the words offered no comfort, only another glimpse at that plate-glass window between her and her family—grown even thicker.

She thought about the twins' brat act. She'd rather work with Patches, the new horse she was training, at his most obnoxious any day. What had her mother gotten them into? DJ sighed. At least she would have one last whole week at Gran's by herself. No other kids in sight.

"Come on, Darla Jean." Gran tapped her grandaughter's arm. "Back to the real world." She smoothed a strand of honey-rich hair back up into the circlet of pink rosebuds that crowned DJ's head. With the sides of her hair caught up in combs and curling down her back, DJ knew she looked almost grown-up, or was it more like a girl in general? She'd been surprised herself when she looked in the mirror. Not a zit in sight, and the bit of eyeshadow and mascara her mother had added to DJ's green eyes had made them sparkle.

Gran slid her arm around DJ's waist. "You looked so grown-up and lovely today, it made me cry. That and the wedding. I sure am glad the boys mananged to hold off that bug until after the ceremony. Kids come down with things so quickly."

"You really think that's what it was? Not just a brat fit?"

"You'd know if you'd felt their foreheads." Gran looked deeply into DJ's eyes. "Darlin', what's bothering you?" Typical Gran—she always knew.

DJ started to shake her head, but Gran's squint caught her. The squint said, *Come clean, kid.*

Joe came up behind Gran and put his hands on her shoulders. "What's up?" He, too, looked at DJ as if analyzing her expression.

They waited.

DJ shifted from one pinched foot to the other. Maybe things would feel better if she took her shoes off. She did so, holding up one offending low-heeled pump. "These."

Gran shook her head, just enough to be noticeable. She leaned back, resting against Joe's broad chest.

"And?"

DJ bit her lip, then rolled the bottom one up over the top. She stared at the shoe in her hand. "She didn't even hug me good-bye." The words hung in the air. DJ could feel the burning behind her eyes as her nose started to run. *You are not going to cry. Get real! One less hug is no big deal. This isn't the first time your mother didn't hug you.*

She sniffed.

"Oh, darlin'." Joe and Gran wrapped her in their arms, just like she was the middle of a sandwich and they were the bread. "It was only an oversight. Lindy's not used to dealing with sick boys, either. And you handle everything so well that . . ."

"That she just forgot." Joe finished the sentence. "It doesn't mean she loves you any less."

"But it hurts just as bad . . . right?" Gran tipped DJ's chin up so she could see her eyes. "I'm glad to know there have been enough hugs between the two of you lately that you miss one."

DJ nodded. Being the middle of a sandwich felt mighty good right now.

"DJ, sorry to interrupt, but we need to get going." Brad Atwood, DJ's real—or rather biological—father, spoke from behind Joe.

"Thanks." DJ hugged each of her grandparents and took a deep breath. With her smile back in place, she turned to Brad and his wife, Jackie.

"Sure wish you could come home with us," Jackie said. "Stormy misses you." Storm Clouds was the Arabian filly

DJ had fought to keep alive during the flood at her father's horse ranch a few weeks earlier.

"Maybe next weekend?" DJ glanced at Gran to catch a headshake. "Or the next."

"I'll call you." Brad wrapped an arm around her shoulders. "You sure do look lovely, all dressed up like this. When you walked down that aisle, both Jackie and I sniffed back tears."

"You look just as good in jeans." Jackie gave her a hug. "But please make sure we get a picture of you in your outfit. I took some myself, but the photographers always do a better job."

DJ could feel her neck growing hot. She hugged them both again and watched them walk off to the Land Rover. Jackie had her arm through Brad's and was laughing up at him. Talk about an awesome couple. Strange how God worked out the mess created when Brad first called DJ a couple of months ago to introduce himself. He was turning out to be a pretty cool dad after all. How come looking back made it easier to see God at work than looking forward? That was a question she'd have to ask Gran.

DJ slipped on her shoes again and headed back into the stucco building to help collect the presents and visit with her relatives. "I'm coming," she called in answer to her cousin Shawna's beckoning wave. "But I've got to get these shoes off first."

She didn't just change her shoes. Stripping off the dress, she hung and straightened it on the padded hanger, then ran a finger down the satin fabric. It felt almost as good as a newly washed show horse.

"Get a move on, kid," Andy called from the hall.

"Coming." DJ pulled on her dress pants and buttoned her shirt. A sigh of relief escaped when she slid her feet into her tennis shoes. *Back to real life*.

With the whole family pitching in, the mountain of

wrapped packages soon filled two vans, leaving barely enough room for the passengers. Once the caterers had the leftovers boxed and in the back of Joe's Explorer, they all caravaned to DJ's house. Leaving the presents mounded in the family room, the people—and food—headed for Gran and Joe's.

"You think we can go over to the Academy later?" nine-year-old Shawna asked. She and DJ occupied the backseat of Joe's car.

"Sure. I have to feed the horses."

"I . . . I meant to ride," Shawna added. "If you don't mind, that is."

"DJ, quit teasing the girl." Joe grinned at them from the rearview mirror. "Of course you can ride, kiddo. Major needs some extra exercise."

"You sure are free in loaning out *my* horse." Major had been Joe's mount in the San Francisco Police Mounted Patrol, and DJ bought him when Joe retired.

"I can put her up on Ranger."

"Sure, and let her get dumped." DJ turned to Shawna. "You should have seen Joe chew dirt last week. And good old Ranger took off, racing around the arena. Good thing we weren't out on the trail. That horse would still be running."

Joe rotated his shoulder. "Yeah, I can still feel it. But he'd have gone back to the barn. He knows where the feed bucket lives."

"I wouldn't bet on it. That horse is one doughnut short of a dozen."

"Or maybe two." Shawna giggled along with DJ's grin.

"All right, all *three* of my children," Gran joined in.

"Why is everybody picking on me?" Joe winked in the rearview mirror. He parked the car in front of where the garage used to be, before the fir tree crashed onto it during a storm. Getting out, he shouted, "Andy, come protect your old man. These females are ganging up on me."

"Fight your own battles—that's what you always told me."

"You want any help, ladies?" Sonja, Andy's wife and Shawna's mother, called.

Still teasing and laughing, they all picked up the plastic-wrapped trays, boxes of supplies, and container holding the leftover cake and trooped into the house.

"I think we ordered too much food." Gran surveyed her oak table now hidden beneath the stack. Boxes nearly covered the delft blue counter tops, too, and some perched on the stools with blue-and-white print cushions. Like Gran herself, the kitchen always welcomed guests with food and comfort. And right now there was plenty to eat.

"Told you so." Joe sidestepped her poking elbow.

"Sure, after we got to the reception. Where were you when the ordering was going on?"

"As far away as possible." He handed Sonja two of the trays so she could find a place for them in the refrigerator.

"We're going to the Academy," DJ said from the door, where she was pulling on her boots. "See ya."

"You want a ride?" Andy asked.

"Nope, that's what feet are for." DJ stopped at the door. "You can come pick us up if you want. Unless, of course, Joe can find the energy to come take care of his horse. What with his sore shoulder and all." The two girls ducked out the door, the dish towel Joe threw missing them by inches. "You missed!" DJ yelled back.

After jogging the mile to the Briones Riding Academy, DJ and Shawna groomed the horses in double time and before long were walking Major and Patches around the covered and lighted arena. Across the parking lot, the long, low red stables nestled against the hill, with outdoor stalls stairstepping the grade behind. The Briones Academy was home to horses and riders of every caliber, from beginning kids to adults wanting a refresher, from hobby riders to those like DJ who dreamed of the big time.

"Cool it, horse," DJ commanded. Patches twitched his tail and flicked his ears back and forth. DJ made him halt. "You keep going, Shawna. Just remember all you've learned in the past."

"I know, heels down, back straight, hands relaxed but in contact with his mouth."

DJ looked up to catch the proud look on her cousin's face. "Right you are."

Patches shifted from one front foot to the other. His tail swished from side to side.

"He's not very happy, is he?" Shawna asked.

"No, he's being a brat. And, horse, I've had it up to my eyebrows with brats today." DJ tightened the reins. "You are going to stand here until you can behave." When his ears finally pointed forward, DJ squeezed her legs, making sure she was settled deep in the saddle. They circled the ring a couple of times at the walk, then DJ signaled a jog.

Patches pulled at the bit but otherwise settled down, ears checking out the other horses in the ring, the sunshine-and-shadow patterns on the sand, a sparrow cheeping from the rafters above.

"Your rising trot is looking good." DJ jogged up even with the trotting Major.

"Major is such a cool horse. You think he knows I'm a beginner and is being extra nice for me?"

"Yup, he knows you're a beginner and nope, he's that way for everyone. Just like Joe, Major likes to take care of people." DJ smiled at Shawna.

Without warning, Patches arched his back, turning bronc before DJ could stop him. Her seat lost contact with the saddle, and she flew up into the air. "Fiddle!"

2

DJ SLAMMED BACK INTO the saddle and clamped her knees tight.

Patches snorted, fighting to get his head down.

"You are not going to dump me this time!" Teeth clenched, DJ hauled on the reins. Maybe whoever rode this fool horse should take lessons in bronc riding before mounting him. She always told his owner, Mrs. Johnson, to put him on the hot walker first to take the edge off his energy. Maybe she should have taken her own advice.

Within two hops, she had him moving forward again.

"DJ, you all right?" Shawna asked.

"Yeah, I am, but this broomtail isn't." She kept contact with Patches' mouth, her legs and seat driving him forward. How did he know the exact moment she shifted her attention? Did he have eyes in those constantly moving ears of his? All she'd done was look over at Shawna.

Patches kept his ears flat against his head, his tail doing the double twitch. He attempted a sidestep, but DJ knew his tricks and kept him in a forward motion.

"No, you can't lope until you can behave at a jog. Loping is a reward for good behavior."

Patches' ears now flicked back and forth. He let out extra air with a whoosh and settled into a ground-eating, relaxed walk.

DJ let out a matching sigh and allowed herself to enjoy the ride. "How am I ever going to calm you enough for your owner to ride?" she asked. "You pull one like that on her again, and she'll send you to the dog food factory."

"Would she really?" Shawna asked, concern wrinkling her forehead.

DJ shrugged. "Would serve him right—wouldn't it, you broomtail, you." After patting Patches' already sweat-dotted neck, DJ dared to glance at Shawna. "He just has to test his rider, make sure she knows who's in charge. He'll settle down as he gets older. I hope." She patted Patches' neck with one hand again, keeping the other securely on the reins. "He's smart, learns fast when he wants to, and is comfortable to ride. I've got to start taking him up in the park so he learns trail-riding. The Johnsons want to ride as a family."

"I'd sure like that. Wish my mom and dad wanted to ride."

"How do you know they don't?" DJ squeezed her legs just enough to signal Patches he could jog now. They circled the ring, with DJ giving Shawna suggestions on riding skills, reminding her to watch her aids. If DJ didn't know better, she'd think she'd turned into a clone of Bridget Sommersby, their teaching sounded so much the same. Bridget, once a world-class contender in jumping, owned Briones Riding Academy and trained both horses and riders of all levels.

"There's so much to think about, I forget some things." Shawna straightened her back and lowered her heels.

"I know, but it gets easier. For the little you've ridden, you do great."

An ear-to-ear grin split Shawna's face. "Thanks."

After DJ set Shawna to trotting around the ring, then turning and going the other way, she worked Patches through figure eights at both a jog and a lope, halts, backing up, and standing still. The last was the hardest. At least he would stand still now for mounting and dismounting, which she did several times.

Other riders called greetings, with Tony Andrada teasing her about bronc riding. When Tony first came to the Academy, he'd been such a jerk that DJ still found herself wondering who this new person was. DJ had drawn a portrait of Tony's horse when she drew his name for the academy Christmas party, and Tony reminded her every once in a while how much he liked the picture.

DJ mounted for the third time and trotted diagonally across the arena to catch up with Shawna. "You about ready to call it a day?"

"If we have to. I wish I never had to quit."

"You'd get a mighty sore rear, riding all the time."

"DJ! You know what I mean." Shawna stopped Major by the gate. "Hi, Grandpa Joe. When did you get here?"

"Not in time to ride with you two. But Ranger is fed, and some nice person took care of food for this old horse, too." He stroked Major's nose and up around his ears. "Did he behave for you?"

"Sure. I had the greatest time."

"She says she wants to ride forever." DJ leaned forward to open the gate, something she'd risked only a time or two with Patches. His tail swished, but other than that, he held steady.

"Would tomorrow be soon enough? As far as Gran and I are concerned, you're welcome to spend the night. Maybe if the weather stays decent, we can ride up into Briones State Park."

"You mean it?" The younger girl rode through the gate after Patches and DJ.

But when DJ tried to close the gate from Patches' back, the horse shook his head, and instead of going forward, he backed up. When DJ tried to close it again, he sidled away, snorting at the gate as if he'd never seen one his entire life.

DJ tried again, but when Patches still refused, she turned back to trot another round of the arena.

"Come on, let's go feed this old boy." Joe headed Shawna toward the barn. "She might be a while."

But without an audience, Patches gave up. Once he'd allowed her to close the gate without a fuss, DJ took him back to the barn.

Later, back at Gran's, Shawna asked her mom and dad if she could spend the night. When they agreed, she flung her arms around Andy's neck. "Thank you, thank you, thank you!"

"Easy, I can't come get you with a broken neck." Her father hugged her back and tugged her down on the sofa between Sonja and him. "So how'd the ride go?"

"We going to eat soon?" DJ asked, wandering into the kitchen as Shawna began to tell her parents all about it.

"I know, you're starved," Julia Gregory, Joe's daughter, said with a laugh. "You must be a teenager."

"Yup. Gran says I have a hollow leg." DJ raised her right knee. "It's this one, I think."

Julia sighed. "You know, it's just not fair. You eat whatever you want and never gain an ounce, and I just look at a hot fudge sundae and an inch blossoms around my hips."

"I wouldn't mind a couple of inches in some places." DJ snagged a chicken wing from the platter Gran set on the table.

"Don't rush it. The tall, willowy type like you will always be in style." Julia studied DJ with a smile. "I'd give anything for a swan neck like yours." She pulled at the neck of her mock-turtle shirt. "Oh to be able to wear a *real* turtleneck without looking like a turtle."

Willowy? Me? DJ stopped chewing on the chicken wing. *Flat is more like it.* She kept the thoughts from becoming words and glanced over at Gran. She wore that I-told-you-so look that bugged DJ to no end.

"Don't say it." She waved the chicken bone at her grandmother.

"I didn't." Gran held up her hands.

"No, but you were thinking it."

"Can't help thinking the truth."

While DJ frequently complained about being flat front and back, both Gran and her mother told her to quit griping.

"I sure wish my girls could have come along," Julia said with a sigh. "They don't know how much fun having cousins around can be. By the way, DJ, Allison thinks you can walk on water. You got to be her hero when we were here for Thanksgiving."

"Just because I can ride a horse?"

"Well, that, too, but you gave her a ride and paid attention to her. Doesn't take much, you know."

"She's a neat little kid." DJ didn't mention Meredith, Julia's oldest girl, who'd been a royal pain in the patootie. She let everyone know she'd only come because her mother made her. And she wasn't happy about it—or about anything else.

"Living clear across the country like we do makes it hard to feel like part of the family. The girls don't even have the chance to really know their grandparents."

"They're missing out. Gran and GJ are the best."

"GJ? Oh, I get it." Julia smacked the flat of her hand against her forehead. "Grandpa Joe. We've got DJ and GJ. C-l-e-v-e-r."

DJ liked both Julia and her husband, Martin, from even the little time she'd spent with them. "It would be neat if Allison could come stay awhile this summer. Maybe by then the boys will have a pony."

"Or two," Gran added. "Darlin', go call the others to come eat."

Shawna came spinning through the doorway just as DJ turned to round up the crowd. "Guess what? Dad says we might move out here to the country. By you guys! Wouldn't that be the most awesome thing?

"And he said I could take riding lessons on Saturdays from DJ if she wants to teach me so I can ride better, and he said he always thought he might like to ride, too, and we could all go riding up in the park and . . ." She finally had to pause for a breath. "So would you . . . I mean, could you? I mean—oh, DJ!" Shawna leaned against the wall. "Maybe I'll really get to have a horse of my own, just like you do."

"That would be awesome, all right." DJ thought of the discussions she'd had with Amy Yamamoto, her all-time best friend, about cutting back on some things so she didn't feel pressured all the time. Teaching Shawna would certainly add to the load. "But you have to check with Bridget first. Remember, she owns the Academy."

Andy joined them, planting both hands on Shawna's shoulders and drawing her back against him. "We'd pay you for the lessons, just like everyone else. And, yes, I understand we have to go through Ms. Sommersby. Are you sure you have time for another student?"

"Shawna's doing so well that with some more private lessons, she could maybe join my other girls. She'd like the others, even though they ride Western. Come on out to watch a class sometime and see what you think."

"Please, Dad, Mom, can we?"

"We'll see."

"That means yes." Shawna nodded at DJ.

Her father swatted her on the seat. "Let's go eat. Gotta keep up our strength for all this horse stuff."

After the meal, DJ brought out her small sketch pad and took her place again. Everyone sat around the table, picking at the leftover treats and sharing stories they remembered from the past. While she listened and at times contributed stories of her own, DJ drew two nearly identical pictures of a colt peering out from behind the veil of her mother's tail. She added the diamond between the eyes and a line down to a smaller one on the baby's nose. She signed it *Storm Clouds by DJ Randall* and gave one to Shawna.

"Here, give this to Allison," she said, handing the other to Julia.

"You couldn't give her anything to make her happier." Julia held it up for all to see. "I knew you were an artist, but, DJ, you're only fourteen. This is amazing. What an incredible talent you have."

"I have a good teacher." DJ nodded toward Gran.

"Just say thank you, darlin'. God gave you the talent—I just helped mold it a bit." Gran beamed the kind of smile that warmed DJ clear down to her toes.

"You *are* taking art classes, aren't you?" Julia continued to study the pencil drawing. "I can't believe how you can catch such personality like this. That baby just sparks with mischief, yet the whole picture is of utter peace. I swear I can even smell the hay and the horses."

DJ could feel her neck heating up. The urge to chew on her fingernails made her hide her hands under her thighs.

"I'm going to frame this before Allison sees it. I seem to remember you did note cards, too. Do you have any more of them?"

DJ shook her head. "But it wouldn't take long to print some."

"You ever thought about putting them in card shops—the packets of note cards, I mean?" Julia looked up from studying the picture to gaze at DJ.

DJ shrugged. "Not really. Bridget carried them in the tack shop at the Academy, and they went pretty fast. Guess Amy and I kinda forgot about them after Christmas and all.

She had some of her photographs on hers."

"I remember." Julia nodded and nibbled on the side of her lower lip. "If I could get a friend of mine to stock these in her shop, could you produce enough?"

"I guess. How many?"

Sonja leaned forward to scoop dip with a rippled chip. "I bet I could sell some where I work, too. I used the ones you gave me as thank-you cards and got raves about them."

"Let me check into it." Julia turned to Gran. "Do you have any file folders or an envelope I could put this in?" Her eyebrows flicked upward as she asked DJ, "Could I show my friend this one, too?" She motioned with the drawing still held in her hand.

"Sure."

Julia and her husband reluctantly said good-bye when the clock in the living room bonged ten times. After spending the night at DJ's house, they would fly home early Sunday morning. "You'll hear from me soon," Julia promised after giving DJ a big hug. "I am so proud to know you. That big brother of mine got a real gold mine when he found you and your mother."

"Thanks." DJ hugged her back. "Thanks a lot."

Shawna's parents left soon after, with promises to see them the next day.

"You're going to be a famous horse artist one day," Shawna said later from the sleeping bag spread beside the bed. "And I got one of your early pictures. That is so cool."

DJ grinned and reached down to tousle the girl's hair. "You are cool yourself. Sleep fast."

"So we can ride up in Briones! I can't wait."

Possibilities raced through DJ's head. What if the cards sold well? What if they didn't? Wouldn't it be fun to make more? Wait till she told Amy about *this*!

She thought, too, about the way Shawna and her dad could talk and tease each other. Maybe she *had* been missing out on something by not having a father all these years. She turned over and tucked the comforter more tightly around her shoulders. Well, now she was going to—no, change that—she now had *two* fathers. And while the newest one had forgotten to hug her good-bye, the other sure hadn't.

DJ fell asleep while thanking God for the filly who waited for her at Brad's farm and for the chance to ride up in Briones after church in the morning.

Shawna could hardly sit still through church. While clouds had covered the sky when she, Joe, and DJ went to feed the horses, sun now painted the shiny floor with reds and oranges and browns from the stained-glass windows.

"Are you going to ride Patches?" she whispered at one point.

DJ shook her head. "I'll saddle Bandit for you." The gray pony's owner had said she could use their pony any time. She was already using him for little Andrew Johnson's lessons.

Gran gave them a look.

When Shawna started to whisper something else, DJ shook her head.

Was the sermon awfully long, or was she feeling as antsy as Shawna, who couldn't sit still on the pew beside her? DJ refocused her attention on the pastor for the who-knew-how-manyeth time. But whatever he was preaching about didn't make it past her rampaging thoughts. She took in a deep breath and let it all out, dropping her shoulders as she did.

"God, the perfect Father, loves us, loves you, loves me,

right now. No matter what we do, He loves us. Think of that. He loves you." Each word the pastor said now rang and echoed in DJ's head. "God loves you. Yesterday, today, tomorrow. God loves you. Jesus loves you." In a voice rich with love, the pastor emphasized each word. They seemed to fill the sanctuary, bouncing off the beams overhead and dancing with the sun streaming in the window. The precious words circled DJ's heart, invaded it, and took sanctuary there.

"Amen."

DJ heard sniffs and throat clearings from those around her. She wiped away her own tear before it left the haven of her lashes. Gran took a tissue from her purse, and Joe blew into his white handkerchief.

"Awesome," Shawna whispered.

DJ's throat kept closing during the final hymn.

There wasn't a lot of talking as the congregation left the building. GJ wrapped an arm around Gran and the other around DJ as Gran snuggled Shawna close to her side. The four of them walked to the parking lot and the waiting car.

"DJ, wait up!" Amy dashed across the parking lot. She greeted them all, then asked, "You going to the Academy this afternoon?" Her black hair gleamed in the sunlight.

"We're going to Briones," Shawna announced.

"You want to come?" DJ asked.

"You bet I do!" Amy waved at her mother's call. "Just don't leave without me." She darted back between the cars to the Yamamoto minivan.

"You want to eat lunch now, pack a lunch, or ride first and eat later?" Gran asked when they got home.

"Could we pack it?" Shawna asked as if she were being offered a trip to Disneyland.

Gran hugged her on the way up the pansy-bordered

walk. "In a heartbeat. I'll do that while you change clothes. Don't worry, DJ, I'll pack for Amy, too."

"Melanie, my love, you are the best grandma ever," DJ heard Joe say as she headed for her bedroom. DJ totally agreed.

With their lunches in Joe's saddlebags and the horses groomed in record time, the four closed the gates behind them and headed up the trail to Briones State Park. The trail curved around a rounded hill and below a grandfather oak tree raising dark arms against the sun. The hurt-your-eyes green of the grass said that while the calendar still proclaimed winter, the earth on these California hills was thinking spring. The breeze bending the grass held a nip to it when it kissed DJ's cheeks.

She raised her face to the sun and inhaled. "How come new grass smells almost as good as horse?"

A red-tailed hawk, riding the thermals above them, screeched an answer. One of the horses snorted. The saddles creaked and bits jangled, adding a tune all their own.

DJ knew there was no place in the entire world she'd rather be than right here, right now.

They ate their lunch by the fenced-in pond in the upper meadow. Riders on cross-country bikes sped by on the fire road, and hikers whistled for their dogs to keep them from chasing the cows with their calves that grazed the hillsides.

Shawna flung herself on her back, her arms outstretched. "This is a five-million-percent perfect day."

"You said it, kid." Joe balled his sandwich bag and stuffed the trash in his saddlebag. The horses grazed beside them. While DJ told Amy about Julia's offer to take their cards to a gift shop, maybe reproducing one of the filly pictures, too, Joe answered Shawna's stream of questions. They mounted their horses again and rode farther up the hill, following the trails along the ridge until Joe finally said they should head back.

When Shawna groaned, he laughed. "You're going to feel all this tomorrow as it is, young lady. Besides, Gran needs our company."

"When are you going to get Gran a horse?" DJ asked.

"Any time she wants one."

"Just get one, and once we drag her up here the first time, she'll be hooked for sure." DJ thought a moment. "If I can get Patches to behave on the trails, she can ride Major." The tall, dark bay flicked his ears at the sound of his name. DJ patted his neck. Right now she felt like hugging him and the whole world.

"You'd help me find her a horse?" Joe questioned.

"Need you ask? So will Bridget."

"Don't tell her."

"I won't, but we'd better get to work. Mother's Day will be here before you know it."

Joe nodded, a sneaky smile curving his lips. "Thanks, DJ. That's the perfect idea."

When they got home, Andy sat in his car, waiting for his daughter.

"Why didn't you go in the house?" Joe asked.

"It's locked. Besides, I only just got here. Let's get your stuff, Shawna. I need to get back."

When they entered the kitchen, a note on the table said Gran had gone into the city to pick up the twins. Maria had caught the bug, too, and was too ill herself to care for two sick boys.

DJ and Joe waved good-bye to the others a few minutes later. *What are we in for now?* DJ wondered.

3

SO MUCH FOR MY TIME ALONE with *Joe and Gran*.
DJ buried the thought.

Joe leaned down and opened the oven door. "Leave it to
Mel, she has dinner in the oven." The fragrance of roast
beef flanked by onions and garlic floated past DJ's nose.

Her stomach rumbled in anticipation. *Be happy they are
coming*, she told herself. *After all, they're your brothers now*.
A sneaky little voice chimed in, *And now you'll never be able
to send them home*. DJ rubbed a rough spot on her lower
lip with her tongue. When she swallowed, she discovered
another rough spot . . . on the back of her throat. *Great!*
She swallowed again to test out her theory. *The Bs probably
gave their germs to me. That's all I need*.

"You want something to drink?" Joe sounded muffled
since he had his head in the refrigerator.

"Sure. Anything."

A hand came from around the door and handed her a
strawberry kiwi soda. "You hungry?" The rest of Joe appeared, cheese and celery in hand, and he headed for the
sink. "I make great stuffed celery. You want pimento or ol-
ive?"

"Both."

"Me too—why choose when they're both so good." He

stripped a couple of celery stalks off the bunch and handed them to her to wash while he put the remainder of the celery away.

"How come we're having these instead of cookies?"

"Mel's got me on a no-sweets program."

"So she didn't bake cookies?"

He grinned at her while he opened the cheese jars. "Those are for the grandkids. I'm under strict orders."

"I'm a grandkid." DJ dried the celery stalks with a paper towel.

"I know that, but if I have to have celery, you wouldn't be so cruel as to eat cookies in front of me."

"You could always turn your back." She eyed the teddy bear cookie jar.

"You're heartless, you know that?" He plunked the lids back on the cheeses and handed them to her. "Put these away, p-u-lease."

DJ did as he asked. Standing at the refrigerator door, she read the note held there by the teddy bear magnet she had given Gran for Christmas one year. "You know you're supposed to scrub the carrots and potatoes and put them in with the roast—an hour ago."

Joe flinched. "How'd I miss that?" He crunched into his stalk of celery and handed DJ half of each kind. "You gonna help me?"

"What's it worth to you?"

Joe crinkled up his eyes like he was thinking hard. "It's worth you not having to set the table and load the dishwasher by yourself."

"Gran would help me."

"I have a feeling Gran is going to be pretty busy with two sick little boys."

"Did you have to remind me?" DJ picked up the vegetable brush and attacked the red potatoes Joe poured into the sink.

"You have a problem with that?" Joe brought out a bag of carrots and began peeling them.

"No."

"Sounds like a yes to me." He dumped a peeled carrot in with the scrubbed potatoes.

DJ glared at the potato in her hand and scrubbed so hard the red came off.

"So?"

"I really like the boys."

"And?" When she didn't answer, he added, "But?"

"They take so much time and they are so . . . so hyper."

"Maybe it seems that way, but they're really more busy and active than hyper. You just haven't been around little kids much, and those two are a double handful."

"I guess."

"Now, what's really bugging you?" Joe finished peeling the carrots and washed his hands. "Hand me the butcher knife, will you?" He quartered the carrots and potatoes, the knife blade slamming into the cutting board.

"Nothing, forget it."

"Nope. Let's get it out—now."

DJ chewed on her lip. "I . . . I feel like a creep."

"Why?"

"I don't know." She pushed herself away from the counter.

"Not so fast." Joe snagged her arm with one wet hand, leaving a print on the arm of her gray sweat shirt. "Give, girl. This is GJ, remember? I've interrogated hardened criminals. One confused teenage girl, especially my grand-daughter, is a piece of cake."

He handed her the bowl of veggies and, opening the oven door, pulled out the roaster. With the lid open and steam rising, he ordered, "Dump 'em in."

DJ did as asked. "I'm too old to be jealous of two little

boys, sick ones at that." The words gushed as if from a wide open faucet.

"You're a better man—excuse me, woman—than I am, then, because I feel jealous over the kids or even Mel's painting at times."

"You do?" DJ's eyebrows shot up.

"Sure, we all do. Only some, like you, are honest about it bothering you. Most grown-ups have just learned to hide their jealousy and suffer in silence. Some even make the other person miserable by getting even or making smart, cutting comments." He closed the oven door.

"But I thought Christians weren't supposed to feel jealous or mad or—"

"Get even or say things to hurt another's feelings or all kinds of things. Of course we're not supposed to, but sometimes we do. We're human, and we have feelings. But the sin is acting on those feelings. Feelings are neither good nor bad—they just are. It's when you let them take root and begin to poison your mind and soul that you get into trouble." Joe leaned against the counter, waving his celery stalk for emphasis. "There are times when you'll have feelings or thoughts that aren't the best, but let them go. Saying 'I feel really angry' is like popping the top on a can of soda. It lets the fizz out. When Robert was your age, I gave him a punching bag so he could beat his anger out on that rather than on his sister and brother. It helped—a lot."

"Robert got mad?"

"He had a terrible temper."

"Are we talking about the same Robert—you know, the man who married my mother?"

"We sure are. If he gets mad at you, he'll tell you about it. But if he hadn't learned to feel the feelings and then let them go, he wouldn't be where he is today. He's an effective leader and boss because he can control his temper. And let me tell you, there have been plenty of times in his life to test that out." Joe crossed one leg over the other as he nibbled the last bite. He nodded. "I'm really proud of that man. And thank God He answered our prayers. His mother and I spent plenty of time praying for Robert and his temper."

DJ, in a matching pose, nodded beside him. "I was just looking forward to time alone with you and Gran." She forced the words past the rough spot in her throat.

"Thanks for telling me." Joe uncrossed his arms and slid one around her shoulders, drawing her closer to his side. "Bet you miss Gran a lot at times."

DJ nodded. The words wouldn't come this time, but the tears tried to.

"Well, I'll tell you something. I am so grateful she married me, and I couldn't love you more if I'd met you the day you were born." He paused and cleared his throat. "So I'll try to be sensitive to when you two need each other all to yourselves and make sure you get that time. And I'll try hard not to be jealous, but it won't be easy."

DJ leaned her head against his shoulder. "Th-thank you." She sniffed. "You got a tissue anywhere nearby?"

He snagged two from the box on the windowsill. "Here." Giving her one, he used the other. When they'd both blown their noses and wiped their eyes, they paused. Sure enough, a car door slammed.

"I better go help her."

"Me too." DJ followed him out the door.

Bobby and Billy were scrubbing their eyes awake when they opened the back doors to the minivan. Joe picked up one pajama-clad boy and DJ the other so Gran could bring in the suitcase.

"Bobby or Billy?" DJ whispered to the boy with his head on her shoulder.

"Bobby," he croaked back.

Inside, when she tried to set him down, he clung to her with both arms and legs.

"You want to go to bed?"

He shook his head once and hung on.

DJ followed Gran and Joe down the hall and into the guest room with twin beds that the boys called their room. With cowboy bedspreads, minibikes, and a basket of balls, bats, baseball gloves, and dump trucks in the corner, the room certainly looked like a boys' lair. Gran had already taken the twins' matching monkeys out of the suitcase and laid them on the pillows of the turned-back beds. Joe and DJ set their burdens down and tucked the blankets around the sleepy boys. Each with an arm over a monkey, the two turned on their sides and instantly fell back to sleep.

Once in the kitchen, Gran shook her head. "At least Maria got them to the emergency clinic early this morning. The doctor said it looks like strep throat, and they both have congestion in their chests, too. She got them on antibiotics and had the doctor take a look at her, too, since she already felt terrible. By the time I arrived, she was coughing her head off and running a temp. Good thing she called me when she did."

"So who's taking care of Maria?" Joe asked.

"Her sister is going to check on her. I'll call her again first thing in the morning. We could always make up a bed for her here if we need to." Gran rubbed her temples with the tips of her fingers.

"You okay?" DJ asked.

"Just a headache." Gran blew out a breath. "Are the potatoes and carrots done, do you think?"

"Ahh, probably not quite yet." Joe made a face. "How about I make you and DJ a cup of tea and you go put your feet up on the hassock." He turned to the cupboard. "What kind do you want?"

"Orange spice." Gran glanced DJ a question.

"Fine."

As soon as Gran sat in her new wing chair—she now

had one at each house—DJ pulled the matching hassock over, let Gran get comfortable, then took her place on the floor beside her grandmother.

"How was the ride?"

"Heavenly." DJ leaned her cheek on her grandmother's thigh.

Gran stroked DJ's hair. "I'm glad you had fun."

DJ told her about everything they'd seen and done, with Joe adding bits and pieces when he set their full teacups on the end table and relaxed in his recliner. One of the boys coughed, catching their attention.

"Poor little tykes," Gran said. "When they are sick enough to sleep like this, they must be really sick." She checked her watch. "They need their antibiotics pretty soon and more to drink. I should have gotten fruit juice bars on the way home, but I couldn't take them out of the car. Maria said that's all they've wanted since last night. Good thing Robert didn't realize how sick they were, or he would have postponed the honeymoon."

"He knew you and Joe were near."

"And who knew Maria would catch it, too?"

"Must be pretty contagious stuff." Joe sipped his coffee. "We all better take our vitamin C and some of those herbs you found, Mel."

"I already did." Gran sighed after a sip of tea. "This tastes so good. And the dinner smells wonderful. You want to stab the potatoes, darlin'? See if they're done?"

No one moved. Finally DJ asked, "Who are you talking to?"

"Well, I meant Joe, but if you want to go, feel free. If they're done, I'll come make the gravy."

DJ rose from the floor. "No, no, GJ, don't get up. I'll do it."

He opened one eye. "You talking to me?"

DJ pinched his stocking-clad big toe and ambled into

the kitchen. She could hear Joe and Gran talking in the living room, a comforting sound, like a creek murmuring over pebbles and sand. Feeling like she could give them something back, DJ went ahead and made the gravy. While it simmered, she set the table, including the salad Gran had ready in the refrigerator. She sliced the pot roast and laid the carrots and potatoes on the platter surrounding the meat.

"Come and eat," she said from the doorway.

Both Gran and Joe roused from a doze, blinking themselves awake.

"Ready for the gravy maker?" Gran asked, pushing herself up from the softness of her chair.

"It's all done. If you don't get a move on, it will be cold." DJ cleared her throat.

"You sound like me." Gran patted her granddaughter's cheek as she entered the kitchen. "Oh, how lovely that looks. DJ, what a nice thing to do."

"Thanks, kiddo," Joe said, gripping DJ's shoulder. "You know, Mel," he said as he pulled her chair out for her, "this kid is definitely a keeper."

"Oh, I've known that for fourteen-plus years." Gran winked at DJ, but her brow wrinkled when DJ cleared her throat again. "You have a frog in your throat?"

"Something like that." DJ took a drink from her water glass.

"Well, you better not get what the boys have. The clinic doctor told Maria this is a vicious bug going around this year." She reached her hands out to Joe and DJ. "Let's say grace. DJ?"

DJ cleared her throat again. It felt like a sheet of sandpaper was wedged in there. "For health and strength and daily bread, we give you thanks, O Lord. Thank you for my family, please take care of Mom and Robert, and make Bobby and Billy and Maria better. Thank you for the ride into the park today, too. Amen." She squeezed her grand-parents' hands and reached for the salad bowl. "I don't know if there is enough salt in the gravy, so you better try it first."

Their conversation during dinner was punctuated several times by coughing from the boys' room, but still the twins didn't wake. When they were done eating, Gran laid her napkin on the table and sighed. "I hate to wake them, but they need their medicine. Cough syrup might help, too."

"You go ahead, Mel. I'll do the dishes so DJ can get her homework done."

"I can help." DJ gathered her salad bowl and silver onto her plate and stood.

"Thanks, but no thanks. You already did your share."

"Okay, but remember, I volunteered." DJ set her things on the counter and ambled down the hall to her bedroom. Spreading her books out on the bed, she attacked her history chapter first. After reading that, she made a list of four things she might want to do a term paper on. After an hour on the algebra, she still hadn't finished. And the problems that were done could be right or wrong—she had no idea. How come she had such a horrible time with algebra?

Halfway through her grammar assignment, she felt her chin hit the book. Lifting her head again took all her remaining strength.

Blinking and swallowing hard, she got a drink in the bathroom, donned her nightshirt, and mumbling an apology to her unbrushed teeth, fell into the bed.

When she awoke to the sound of crying some hours later, her head ached and her throat felt like someone had been walking around in it wearing football cleats.

4

"GRAN," DJ CROAKED from the school phone on Monday. "Could you please come and get me?"

"Sure, darlin', one of us will be there in ten minutes. I knew you should have stayed home today." She paused to cough. "Excuse me. Now, don't you go waiting outside in the rain. We'll meet you at the door in front of the office."

"You have to come sign me out." Now it was DJ's turn to cough.

"Will do. At the office, then."

"Thanks." DJ shivered again as she hung up the phone. She wrapped her arms around her middle. *If only I could get warm*. She never had taken her jacket off that morning, and she wished she'd brought gloves. DJ retrieved the rest of her books from her locker and went to tell the vice principal, Ms. Benson, what was happening.

"You look like you should have stayed in bed today." The woman smiled and raised a hand to DJ's forehead. "Good grief, child, you feel like you're freezing!"

DJ nodded. When she cleared her throat, she could finally speak. "All day."

"Well, I'd bet my socks you're running a fever. Thanks for spreading more germs around this germ factory."

"Sorry."

"I know. If all the kids had the perseverance you have, we probably wouldn't have room for them all. How's that horse of yours doing?"

DJ's head had begun to feel like miniature ponies were pounding around it in a circle. "Good. Shows will start in a month or so."

"Why don't you go sit down in that chair before you fall down."

"Thanks." DJ did as suggested and tucked her cold feet up under her. With her hands in her armpits, she still shivered. Just as Joe walked in the door, Ms. Benson brought DJ a blanket.

"Bring this with you when you come back to school, and don't be in too much of a hurry. Get well."

DJ nodded her gratitude and snuggled the blanket around her shoulders. While she was glad none of the kids were around to see her, she was too cold to care if they did.

"That bad, huh?" Joe handed her into the Explorer, where he had left the engine running and the heater on full blast. "I knew I should have insisted you stay home this morning."

"Don't tell me how bad I look, please." DJ poked only her nose out from the blanket. An onset of coughing felt like it tore the lining right off her throat.

"Since the boys have strep, maybe we should take you right to the doctor."

"Please, Joe, I just want to go home to bed."

"I have to warn you, Bobby and Billy are better. They've been on the antibiotic twenty-four hours now, and little kids bounce back quickly."

DJ groaned. "Maybe I should just go home to my own house."

"All by yourself? Not on your life."

Hours later when she woke up, she felt even worse, if that was possible. She drank the hot lemonade Joe brought her, sucked on some throat lozenges, and conked out again. When she woke again, her bed was sweat soaked and so was she. But in spite of all the sweat, DJ couldn't quit shaking. She put on dry pajamas and crawled back under the covers after Joe and Gran changed the bed.

"I'm calling the doctor." Gran stuck a thermometer under DJ's tongue.

DJ shook her head. When she tried to speak around the thing in her mouth, Gran just held up a hand.

"Don't bother to argue. Dr. Jaspers most likely won't want you in his office anyway. If they need a throat culture, I know how to do that. Open your mouth and stick out your tongue." Gran pointed the flashlight into DJ's mouth. "Yuck. He said that both strep throat and the chest flu are going around, plus a nasty combination of both."

The bed tap-danced on the floor, DJ shook so hard. She could hear the boys giggling in their room. If only she got over this as fast as they did. If she didn't die first.

Gran returned in a few minutes. "Amazing, I got right through. Probably because he was ready to go out the door." She sat down on the bed. "Anyway, Joe just went to pick up a prescription and some throat swabs. The doctor said this sounds like what everyone else has, only you got the double whammy."

Gran turned her head away to cough into her hand.

"Hope you told him you've got it, too." DJ's head spun just from talking.

"Not yet, I don't. Just a cold so far and not bad at that. I'm taking care of myself." Gran opened a bottle of pills. "Here, this will help get your temp down."

DJ tried to swallow them, but they stuck at the back of her tongue. She gagged and choked, finally spitting them out again. The room twirled, and Gran turned into two. DJ coughed till it felt like her lungs might come flying out of her mouth.

Gran shook her head. "Well, I haven't had to crush tablets in sugar for you in a long time, but if that's what it takes to get them down, so be it." She handed DJ a juice bar. "Eat this."

Sick as she was, DJ recognized an order when she heard one. Bites of the frozen bar slid past the sore throat amazingly well.

"Drink."

DJ's eyelids had started to close already but flew open at Gran's General Crowder voice. DJ drank, swallowed the sugar mixture from a spoon, then drank again.

She was nearly asleep when Joe returned. Gran sat on the edge of the bed. "Here are the antibiotics. Good thing he put them in small capsules. If you drink plenty of water with them, they should go down."

"Gran, I can't. I'm so dizzy." DJ tried blinking, but the room tilted, and Gran looked to be sliding off the bed.

"Keep your eyes closed." Gran put the pill in DJ's hand, then held her head while she drank. The glass clinked against her teeth when a shudder hit her.

"Good girl, now I'll leave you alone."

DJ mumbled something, but even she wasn't sure what.

"What day is it?"

"Wednesday afternoon." Joe sat down beside her.

"What happened to Tuesday?"

"We skipped it." Joe didn't crack a smile.

"Where's Gran?"

"In bed."

"Same stuff?"

"Hope not. But I sent her to bed so it wouldn't get

worse." He handed her a glass with a straw that bent. When she slid up against the headboard, the room stayed level. "Drink."

She did. He handed her another pill. She swallowed it and drank again. "Thanks, Dr. Joe."

Suddenly, DJ's eyes flew wide open. "Wednesday afternoon! I had classes to teach and—"

"Too bad. Bridget took them. I told her you would probably be out all week."

"All week!"

Joe looked around the room. "We got a parrot in here somewhere?" He patted her hand. "Just go back to sleep and get better. The Bs are missing you."

"Yeah, right. They started all this." DJ scooted back down under the covers and rolled over on her side. "It'll take me a week just to catch up on all my homework."

"You hungry?"

DJ thought a minute. "No."

"Okay, call me if you need anything. I'll be taking the boys up to the Academy with me to feed the horses."

His last remark sounded like he stood a mile away.

Later that evening, Joe came to her door. "You feel up to talking with Amy? She's called every day."

DJ raised up on her elbows. Her window showed only darkness outside. She blinked. "I guess so." Now she sounded like a frog who croaked tenor. After she'd flipped on to her back, Joe handed her the portable phone. "Hi."

"Hope you look better than you sound."

"I guess. Haven't seen a mirror." DJ took the glass of water from her nightstand and sucked on the straw.

"You know half the school is out with strep or the flu? They're calling it an epidemic."

"Uh-huh." DJ rubbed her eyes. She could hear the boys in the kitchen with Joe, asking him their standard million questions.

"You want me to bring you your homework?"

"I guess." *Who cares about homework? Living is the issue.*

"So you feel any better?"

"Better than what? All I do is sleep."

"You'll get better."

DJ tried to think of something to say, but words and ideas failed to creep out of the fog in her head.

"Maybe I should call back tomorrow."

" 'Kay." DJ clicked off the phone. She drank again and decided she needed to use the bathroom. She sat up, and the room spun. She swung her legs over the side of the bed. The room tilted. She stood up. The floor rushed up to meet her. Getting from the floor to the bathroom and back to bed would equal about a fifty-mile run—in the rain—through a flood. DJ laid her cheek against the cool hardwood floor. Her knee hurt.

"My goodness, what happened?" Gran barged through the bedroom door, the boys right on her heels.

DJ straightened her arms and tried to push herself up. Before she could do any more, Joe joined the circus and scooped her up. When he started to put her back in bed, she shook her head and pointed to the bathroom.

"I'll carry you in there, and Gran will help you." His gentle voice tickled her ear.

How freaky can I get? I can't even walk across the room. DJ forced her fingers to let go of Joe's arm when he set her down on the cold bathroom floor. When Gran had her arm around DJ's waist, Joe left the room. "Now that I'm standing, it's not so bad." DJ sucked in a deep breath and prayed the room would stand still. It did.

"It's changing altitudes that make things spin."

"You don't sound so hot yourself."

"The rest helped. And Joe is pretty much taking care of things, especially the boys. If only the rest of us bounced back like they do."

"If only they'd kept their germs to themselves."

"Their father and mother taught them to share."

DJ shook her head. "Bad one, Gran."

By the time she was helped back into bed, given more pills, forced to drink some chicken soup and cough hard, DJ felt like she'd run that fifty miles after all.

"Why make me cough like that?" she groaned.

"So your lungs stay clear. All you need is a bout with pneumonia." Gran rubbed DJ's back now instead of just thumping on it.

"So I should thank you, huh?"

"I know you do, darlin'. It's just that right now, anything feels uncomfortable."

"You think I'll be able to take a shower in the morning and wash my hair?" DJ ran her fingers through the sticky mass.

"We'll see." Gran touched a finger to the tip of DJ's nose. "That means you're feeling better."

"No, just feeling too grossed out to stand myself as is."

After the shower the next day, DJ slept the rest of the morning. But that afternoon, she gave in to the twins' pleading and read them a story. With the three of them propped against the head of her bed and the zany words of Dr. Seuss, DJ even managed to laugh a little. When Amy called that night, they talked for a half hour. Finally caught up on all the news of school and barns, DJ looked at the pile of books by her bed.

"I have no brain left for homework."

The phone rang, but DJ ignored it until Joe called to say it was for her.

"DJ? This is Brad."

"I know. How are things?"

"You sound terrible."

DJ groaned.

"Oops, not a good thing to say, huh?"

"Nope."

"Okay, let's start again. Are you getting sick or getting well?"

"Better be well." DJ told him a little of what she remembered of the last three days.

"Uh-oh. I was hoping you could come up for the weekend. Stormy's been missing you."

"I'll ask Gran."

"No, you won't. I take back the invitation. Maybe we can try for next weekend."

"But—"

"Nope. You've got to get better. If you come up here and have a relapse, your mother will kill me, if Jackie doesn't first."

By the time DJ said good-bye, she felt flatter than a piece of paper. *I could be going up to see the foals, to play with Stormy. Soon, she's not even going to remember me.*

When one of the twins came to her door with another book in hand, she glared at him. It was his fault she got sick. Throwing the book on the bed against the wall seemed like a good idea.

"Brad wanted me to come up there this weekend," she told Gran a bit later.

"And you told him no?"

"No! I was going to ask you, but he took back the invitation."

"Smart man. You can't go visiting when you aren't well enough to go to school."

"I'm going tomorrow."

"I don't think so."

"G-r-a-n."

"No." She shook her head and shrugged. "One more day won't hurt, and it may keep you going next week."

"Then I can't go to the barns!" The groan escalated to a wail.

"You got it."

"If I don't cough all night, can I go?" DJ tried to ignore the tickle in her throat, but the cough finally won out. She coughed till she felt sick to her stomach.

Gran handed her the water glass. "Did you want to start counting any time soon?"

DJ glared at her grandmother. In her wishes to stay at her grandparents' house, she'd forgotten how stubborn Gran could be.

Gran dropped a kiss on DJ's forehead. "Love you, darlin'. Too much to let you get sick again." She shut off the light as she left the room.

By Saturday afternoon, DJ wanted to ship the twins to Siberia or outer Mongolia, whichever was farther away. She knew they couldn't help talking nonstop, but her head rang from it. When she asked them to quit bouncing on her bed, they climbed off and bumped all her school books to the floor. And she'd lost track of the times they asked her to read to them. Couldn't they understand she felt like crud? Outer Mongolia, for sure.

5

IF I HEAR 'DJ!' one more time, I'm going to throw them out the door!

Gran and Joe had gone to the store for groceries, leaving DJ to watch the boys.

DJ had read the boys three books, helped them build a fort with their Legos, and either wiped or reminded them to wipe their noses four hundred and twenty-two times. She quit counting after that. A video of *The Lion King* held their attention—for the moment.

Back to her homework. She studied the list from her English teacher. One journal entry for every day. It had been two weeks since she'd written anything. The journals were due yesterday, but since she'd been home, she'd have to turn it in Monday. One paper using contrast, one on comparison—she'd have to read the chapter first. Another book report was due, too, and she hadn't begun to read another book.

She sighed and took out the history list. Only four chapters to read, then choose a famous person from the middle ages to research and write about. No big deal, right?

Her head started to ache again.

She ignored the algebra book for now. She'd missed a quiz on Wednesday.

She headed for the freezer. A juice bar sounded good. Should she disturb the Double Bs and see if they wanted one? *Nope.*

Not fair! Her little voice plagued her at times. This was one of those times. Sighing, she turned and entered the family room instead. "You guys want a juice bar or Popsicle?"

"Is there purple?"

"I don't know what kind there is. Come choose."

Licking her own strawberry one, she left the boys back in front of the video, purple Popsicles in mouths, napkins in laps, noses wiped—again. *I sure hope Mom and Robert are having a good time. Look at all the fun they're missing out on here.*

She piled the pillows behind her and settled on the bed, history book in hand, note pad beside her knee. Maybe if she hurried, Gran and Joe would let her go feed the horses later. If she could indeed convince Gran she was all better. She coughed and blew her nose. She kept her mind from replaying the fun she was missing by not being with Brad and Jackie. As Gran had reminded her, they didn't need the germs, either.

But DJ hadn't ridden since Sunday and the trail ride into Briones. She stared out the window, past the running rivulets and at the gray sky. Yuck. Back to her homework.

"DJ?"

She groaned. "What?"

"I'm hungry."

"Me too."

"You just had a Popsicle." She finished her juice bar and dropped the stick into the wastebasket by the bed.

"Only half." They appeared at her door. Mouths lined in purple, noses red from the blowing and running. One had his Winnie the Pooh sweat shirt on backward.

DJ groaned again, set her book aside, and followed the

groove she'd worn in the floor back to the kitchen. She split another purple Popsicle and sent them back to the family room.

"Our video is done."

"Push rewind and put in another." The two could work a VCR better than most adults.

"When's Gran coming home?"

DJ paused in the door to her room. "I don't know. Soon." She looked back to see both boys wearing the woeful basset hound look, dark circles under their eyes.

"Will you read us a story?"

"Please?"

"Look, guys, I have a mountain of homework to do, and I don't feel so hot, either. Why don't you each bring a book in here so you can look at the pictures while I study. But you have to be quiet."

What she really wanted to do was take a nap. You'd think she'd been sick for a month, not five days. She plumped up her pillows again and settled a boy on each side of her.

"Now, you promised to be quiet."

"Yes."

The boys read, or rather, looked at the pictures quietly—too quietly. DJ glanced from side to side. They were both sound asleep. A yawn cracked her jaw. Maybe she'd just close her eyes for a second or two to give them a rest from all the studying. Her head bobbed as she dropped off.

The fire crackled and snapped, devouring the wood between her and the open barn door. DJ's skin felt like it was being pulled off her flesh from the heat. She pulled on the lead ropes, but Stormy and her mother refused to leave the stall. A horse screamed. DJ ripped off her shirt and tied it over the mare's eyes. With a breath of prayer, she dove between the flames. God, make them follow!

DJ sat straight up in bed, her heart pounding so hard it

felt like her ribs would crack. She tried to take in a breath—when it wasn't smoke filled, she knew for sure she'd been dreaming. The twin on either side of her squirmed and rolled over. She pushed the quilt back.

There was no fire! Thank God there was no fire! Rubbing the scar in her right palm, she inched toward the end of the bed. No wonder she'd dreamed of fire, with the quilt and the hot bodies beside her, she'd been on fire herself. She rubbed the scar again. If only she could remember the long-ago accident, maybe the nightmares would cease. And maybe she wouldn't freak at the sight of fire.

A drop of sweat ran down her right temple. She gulped the remaining water in the glass on the nightstand and made her way to the bathroom. It took drinking another whole glassful before she could get the feeling of smoke out of her throat. She leaned straight-armed on the counter and stared at the face in the mirror.

"When are you going to get over being so scared of fire?"

The face didn't answer. DJ ran shaky fingers through her hair, pushing it back off her face. Picking up the brush, she worked it through the snarls and, wrapping a scrunchie around the stuff, got it up off her neck. That helped.

"Man, oh man." She pulled her T-shirt away from her chest, turned on the water, and scooped it over her face. She could hear Joe and Gran in the kitchen and wandered out there.

"DJ, what's wrong?" Gran took one look at her and laid the back of her hand against the girl's forehead. "Your temp's back."

"I just had a terrible dream. I couldn't get Stormy and her dam out of a burning barn." The memory of it sent a shiver up her spine.

"When people run fevers, they often have strange dreams." Joe turned from the cupboard where he was putting away groceries.

DJ plunked down on the wooden stool by the phone. "I'm sick of being sick."

"Drink some orange juice." Gran reached for a glass in the cupboard and handed it to her.

"I'm sick of orange juice. All I want is to go see Major."

"I already fed the horses. He asked about you."

"Funny." But she couldn't help smiling—almost.

"So did Tony and Amy and Bridget. Bridget especially hopes to see you soon. She's teaching for one of the others who's out sick, too." Joe raised an eyebrow. "Oh, and Bunny asked after you, too. Said she has something she wants to ask you."

Gran shook her head. "Don't even think it, DJ. You go over there and you'll come home sicker than ever and—"

"I know. And no one else wants my germs." DJ mimicked Gran's tone.

"Maria's sister called. The doctor ordered Maria to the hospital. She has pneumonia *plus* infections in her sinuses and ears. Now *she's* really sick. You want to change places with her?"

DJ shook her head. "Can I call Amy?"

"Sure." Gran turned to Joe. "We really need to go visit Maria tomorrow. Maybe Lindy and Robert could stop on their way out from the airport."

"If they call first." Joe poured himself a glass of water.

Talking to Amy didn't help DJ a whole lot. Only Amy and John hadn't caught the bug at their house. All the rest were sick.

"Do you have a book for me to read? I need to do a book report."

"You want John to bring over a Nancy Drew? If I can get him to, that is."

"I guess."

"Well, don't act too excited."

"Guess it's better than doing algebra."

"So, do you or don't you? You know you'll owe him something if he does it."

"I'll ask Joe." When he agreed, she took the phone off her shoulder. "Joe'll be there in a couple of minutes. Thanks." She hung up the phone and propped her chin on her palms, elbows braced on the counter.

A glass of orange juice clunked on the counter beside her.

"Drink!"

Gran's tone said *now*, so DJ drank.

"You need anything else?" Joe asked on his way out the door.

DJ shook her head. "But thanks." She watched him go. "How can I be tired when I just slept again?" She rubbed her forehead. "Can I get in your bed? The boys have mine."

"They'll be out here in a minute. I just heard them." Gran came and gave DJ a hug. "You'll live, darlin'."

"I know. But this stuff is really the pits." She leaned her forehead against Gran's shoulder.

"I want my daddy." One of the boys shuffled in and leaned against DJ.

The other clutched Gran's apron. "Me too."

DJ reached for the box of tissues and handed them each one. "Blow." She rolled her eyes at Gran and shook her head. "One thing's for sure, I will *never* be a nurse."

By Sunday evening, DJ had all her homework caught up but the book report. She tried skimming the book just enough to do the report but kept getting caught up in it. She filled out the book report form as much as she could and kept on reading.

By 8:00, they still hadn't heard from Lindy and Robert.

"When's my daddy coming?" Both boys looked up at DJ from the floor by her feet.

"Got me." DJ looked to Gran for an answer. If they'd asked once, they'd asked a million times.

"Sometimes planes are late," Gran said. "Why don't you go sit on Grandpa's lap? Maybe he'll read you a story."

"He's sleeping," DJ hissed.

"Oh, you're right." Gran gathered both of the twins close. "You go get a book, and I'll read you a story."

DJ went back to Nancy Drew.

9:00 came and went.

"But I want to stay up and see my daddy," Bobby argued when Gran said it was time for bed.

DJ'd finally figured out a way to tell them apart. She'd put a red shirt on Bobby and a blue one on Billy. They thought it was funny. Even without their color-coded shirts, DJ knew Bobby as the one who argued more.

"How about if I call the airport and see when the plane is arriving?" At Gran's suggestion, their frowns turned upside down. "While I do that, you go get into your pajamas." They scampered out of the room and down the hall. "Daddy's coming, Daddy's coming!" they chanted.

"They've been on the ground for over an hour," Gran announced when she hung up. "They could be here any minute."

Joe checked his watch. "Depends on how long it takes to get their luggage. I'll go dish up some ice cream. Come on, DJ, you can chop the nuts for sundaes."

"Do you have good fudge sauce?" She put the book down and got to her feet, taking time to stretch in the process.

"The best. Mrs. Whatshername's Fudge Sauce."

"You're a good man, Charlie Brown," DJ quoted the last book Gran had read to the boys.

The sundaes had disappeared and another book had

been read when the sound of a car made both boys sit up straight. "Don't need a watchdog with them on guard." Joe let loose so Bobby could slide to the floor. When they heard the car slow down and turn into the driveway, both of them darted to the window. "Daddy's here! Daddy's here!"

DJ breathed a sigh of relief. While she hadn't said anything to anyone, she'd been praying for a safe drive from the airport. She'd heard that most accidents happen within five miles of home.

"Daddy! Daddy!" The twins both would have pelted out the door into the rain if DJ and Joe hadn't grabbed them.

"Sorry we're late," Robert called, helping Lindy out of the car at the same time. "Fog in Los Angeles." Arm in arm, the two came up the walk. The glow from the yard light set haloes of light around them.

The look they gave each other told the whole story. DJ swallowed a lump in her throat. Her mother's face glowed like the streetlights lending iridescent shimmers to the fog.

Robert wore a child on each arm as they all gaggled in the living room.

"We was sick." Bobby put his hands on Robert's cheeks and turned his head so he could look right in his father's eyes.

"Real sick," said the other.

"Nanny Ria is in the horsepistol."

"Horsepistol?" Robert thought a moment. "Oh, the hospital." He turned to his father. "What's been going on?"

"Strep and flu. We all had it and mostly got over it, but they put Maria in the hospital yesterday with pneumonia."

"So you've had the boys since when?"

"Last Sunday afternoon, late. I went in to get them." Gran stood between DJ and Lindy.

"They weren't supposed to come out here until *this* afternoon. I'm sorry, Dad, if I'd known—"

"Nothing you could have done. This whole area's been

under siege. You two didn't get it?"

"No, nothing." Lindy reached for one of the boys and sat down on the sofa with Billy on her lap. "We brought you some presents," she said after kissing his cheek and ruffling his hair. "DJ, could you go get the extra bag out of the trunk?"

"I will." Joe reached for Robert's keys.

DJ snagged a jacket off the hook in the closet and followed him out the door. Again, the boys took center stage. She might as well have not been in the room. But when something needed doing, who did Lindy ask?

Me, that's who. Good old DJ, the walking, talking mule. Good for fetching and carrying, but always easy to ignore. Is this the way life is going to be?

6

DJ STILL HAD A HEADACHE in the morning. Or was it another?

"Bye, honey, I'll call you later."

"Bye, Daddy." The two voices spoke as one.

The door closed on Robert. In a minute, he started his truck and backed out the drive.

On this first morning as a family in their own house, DJ heard it all. She forced her eyes to remain open. No way was she going to stay home from school today. Headache or no, she forced her muscles to move and headed for the bathroom.

"DJ's up! Hi, DJ! You want to play Legos?"

Big mistake. She should have checked to make sure the hall was clear first. "Sorry, guys, I gotta get ready for school."

"We can help."

"No . . . I don't think so."

"Bobby, Billy, your breakfast is ready."

The way miraculously cleared in front of her as the boys pounded down the stairs and into the kitchen. Did they *never* try slow motion?

DJ took a shower and washed her hair. Even that small action made her tired. This looked to be a long day, no two ways about it. She was brushing her teeth when the pounding came on the door.

"We need the bathroom, DJ. You gots to hurry."

DJ groaned. "In a minute." She squeezed toothpaste onto the brush.

"I gotta go."

"Use the other bathroom."

"Can't. Mommy is in there." A hand jiggled the doorknob.

DJ groaned louder. With a mouthful of toothpaste, she pulled her nightshirt back on over her wet hair and opened the door. She went back to scrubbing her teeth but turned when she caught two blue pairs of eyes staring at her. "Now what?" She spit, then caught water in her hand to rinse her mouth.

"You still in here."

She spit out the rinse. "So?"

"So we gotta go." They danced in place.

Groan number three. "Look, guys . . ." She caught the look of distress on their faces and threw up her hands. "Okay, I'll leave." *I've given them baths and dressed them. But now I have to leave.* She shook her head and went to her own room to dress. The day as growing longer instead of shorter.

By the time Lindy dropped DJ off at the high school, her ears were ringing from the constant chatter and her cheek was sticky from the Bs' good-bye kisses. Her mother waved good-bye with a cheerful smile.

"Have a good day, dear."

"Right."

"Bye, DJ! Bye!"

She turned from the curb to catch one of the high-school boys laughing. Was it at her? She could feel the heat in her face, and this time it wasn't from running a temperature.

"Hey, glad to see you could make it." Amy flashed her a grin. She looked again. "What's up?"

"What do you mean?"

"Your face—it's all red."

DJ shook her head. "You don't want to know."

"Sure, I do." Amy switched a couple of things from her backpack to her locker. The warning bell rang. Together they walked toward their homeroom. "So?"

"You're used to little brothers and sisters."

"Yeah?"

"I'm not." DJ sighed. "They are so . . . so busy. They talk all the time, they run up and down the stairs, they need the bathroom, they . . ."

"They fight?"

DJ frowned and shook her head. "I guess not, or at least not much."

"Then you've got it made. Fighting's the worst."

They slipped in through the door just as the final bell rang.

"Would you ladies like to take your seats?" Mr. Deushane arched an eyebrow. "Welcome back, Miss Randall."

The flames fanned her face again. Couldn't he just call her DJ like she asked? But, no, Mr. Deushane called all students by their last names, with a Mister or Miss in front. "Thank you."

"Everyone brought their homework?"

DJ breathed a sigh of relief. She'd gotten all of hers done, even the makeup. She passed her papers forward with the rest of the students. Since they were studying nutrition, she'd drawn the new pyramid for the food groups, adding chocolate in parentheses at the bottom.

When he'd collected all the papers, he handed out one of his own. Sporadic groans rose at the word *quiz* at the top of the paper. "All right, everyone." He raised his hands as if directing a choir. "Together, and on three. One, two, three." Now everyone groaned in sync.

DJ smothered a giggle. While some of the kids made fun of Mr. Deushane behind his back, she thought he was funny, no matter how dull the topic might seem.

When DJ got to art class, she breathed in clay, oil paint, acrylic, glue, paint thinner—all the odors that when mingled together said *art room*. To DJ's mind, the smell of the art room was second-best to horse. Gran's rose water came in a close third.

"You got over the bug, huh?" Mrs. Adams, the teacher, asked. "Glad to see you back." As the others straggled in, she donned her paint-smeared smock and began moving from station to station to check on individual projects. The still life of an empty picture frame, a cylindrical terra cotta pitcher, and a purple silk iris in a clear water glass still graced the top of a draped table. All the students were working in pastels, so the smell of chalk dust tickled DJ's nose, making her sneeze. She took her pad out of her cubbyhole and perched on her stool. Since she'd been gone a whole week, she was just beginning the drawing.

She'd finished roughing in the outlines when Mrs. Adams stopped at her side. "Check the perspective again on that frame. It's off a bit."

DJ stared at the still life, then at her drawing. She erased the top line and squinted to see if hers followed the other angles. Lightly redrawing it, she checked again, using her pencil at a slant for both.

"Good," Mrs. Adams said with a nod and a pat on the shoulder. "If you have time after school one day, you could stay and catch up." She smiled. "I know, you have to get to the Academy."

"I'll try for Wednesday, if that's okay with you."

"Sure. You working on anything at home?"

"I've drawn a couple of my new filly, Storm Clouds." DJ turned on the stool, her heels hooked over the rung. "She is the cutest thing you ever saw. She hides behind her dam—that's the mother. . . ."

At DJ's questioning eyebrow, Mrs. Adams nodded. "Thanks, you know I don't know horse terms."

". . . and peeks around her hind legs, with the dam's tail feathered over her face."

"And you drew that?"

"A couple of times now. My aunt wants to show it to a friend of hers in Connecticut who owns some gift stores. They might want me to make copies for framing and others in note cards—you know, like Amy and I did at Christmas."

"That's wonderful. You know, if you could spend as much time with your art as you do with your horses, you'd . . ." She stepped back with a shrug. "I know, I know, but you can't blame me for trying. You want to jump in the Olympics, and I want you designing the symbols."

"Yeah." But a glow warmed her stomach region.

"You want to bring one in to show me?"

DJ shrugged. "Sure, I'll bring it tomorrow. Why?"

"Well, there's a drawing teacher in San Francisco who has offered to take ten students for a weekend at her home and studio. She chooses them based on what she thinks of application drawings."

"Ten? From all the high schools?" DJ shook her head. "No chance."

"But you'll bring it in and let me enter it if I think it has possibilities?"

DJ shrugged again. "Why not? How much does it cost to enter?"

"Nothing but the postage, and I'll spring for that."

"It's your dime."

"Nothing goes for a dime anymore, DJ." Mrs. Adams wandered off to the next student, leaving DJ concentrating on her still life.

What chance did her foal drawing have when she

couldn't get the perspective right on a silly picture frame?

On the way out of the classroom, she stopped at Mrs. Adams' desk. "Do you know when the art weekend will be?"

"No, why?"

"Well . . . just in case . . . you know . . ."

"In case she chooses you?"

DJ nodded. "If it was a show weekend, I couldn't go."

"When do your shows start?"

"I think the first show is the last weekend in April."

"No problem. I'm sure this was earlier in the month."

"Okay, thanks." DJ hustled and still was late for her PE class.

When she got home from school, DJ felt like falling on the bed and sleeping the night away. Instead, she forced herself to get dressed and ride her bike to the Academy. Pedaling along beside Amy, DJ could feel the sweat start under her arms and on her forehead. At the stop sign, she stopped and leaned her head over the bars, fighting to catch her breath.

"You sure you shouldn't have stayed home?"

"No . . . no . . . I'll be okay." A pain stabbed her right side. She rubbed her ribs, but the pain didn't go away. Ignoring it, she pushed her pedal down and pealed out. Going downhill to the academy drive was easier, and the pain disappeared. Parking her bike beside the barn, she headed to the office.

"DJ, I am so glad you are here." Bridget pushed her chair back and stood. "You are well now?"

"No, she isn't. She should be home." Amy stopped next to DJ. "She's weak as a newborn kitten."

Some friend, DJ thought. *If only she wasn't so right on.*

7

DJ POKED AMY WITH HER ELBOW. "The 'weak' kitten still has claws."

"All right, you two." Bridget shook her head, the glasses she had pushed up on her forehead slipping down with the motion. "DJ, Mrs. Johnson insists she is ready to start training on Patches with your coaching."

DJ groaned. "No, she isn't. Or he isn't."

"I do not think so, either, but she insists and she could be right. She should know herself better than we do."

"True, but I know Patches. And half the time Mrs. Johnson rushes and doesn't take time to put him on the hot walker, so he's just busting with energy when he starts out."

"I've seen DJ on his neck," Amy chimed in.

"And in the dirt." DJ made a face. She pantomimed spitting out dirt.

"Mrs. Johnson will be here in a half hour. You want to put Patches on the hot walker now?"

"Right." DJ kept the groan inside. Bridget frowned on grumbling and forbid excuses.

Bridget studied her notes. "Your three girls are doing very well. You can be proud of them."

"Thanks." A compliment from Bridget ranked up there with purple Grand Champion rosettes. "Anything else?"

"Yes, I might have another green broke horse coming in. She is about the same level as Patches was when you began with him. Would you be interested in taking her on?"

"Sure." Even as she agreed, her mind went into speed mode. *That sure would help with the money situation*. But the cautious side of her mind responded, *Yeah, right, with all the extra time you have already*.

After they'd entered the tack room, Amy said, "That new horse is going to need an hour a day, at least in the beginning." She swung her grooming bucket with one hand.

"I know." DJ rubbed her bottom lip with the tip of her tongue. "But I need the money. I'm about broke again. Major needs shoes, and he's due for worming pretty soon."

"Doesn't the Academy pay you next week?"

"Yeah, but it's never enough."

DJ led a dancing Patches out to the hot walker and clipped him on. "See if you can behave today. Or I swear, I'll pound you into the ground." Patches snorted, spraying her with bits of the horse cookie she had given him. "Yuck."

Major sent her a big-time welcome, nickering and tossing his head. In the next stall, Ranger joined the party. Major leaned as far over the blue web gate as he could, his nostrils fluttering in a soundless nicker. When DJ wrapped her arms around his neck and hugged him, he rested his cheek against hers. "Hi, big guy." Major sighed, a big sigh, and leaned on her shoulder. She rubbed up behind his ears and down his neck.

"I sure missed you." She patted his shoulder and stepped back so she could dig his carrots out of the front pocket of her sweat shirt. While he munched, she retrieved the brushes from her bucket and set about grooming him. "I see your old dad's been here and cleaned out the stalls, huh?"

Major looked over his shoulder as if to agree.

"Sure wish we could ride now, but I have to give a lesson first. Probably should have ridden Patches before Mrs. Johnson gets him, but the hot walker will have to do."

The thought bothered her. Maybe DJ *should* ride him first. If he got his training lesson, then he would be more willing—right? Against her personal desires, she dropped the brushes back in the bucket and, giving Major a last pat, headed for Patches' stall. She left the grooming bucket there and retrieved the horse from the hot walker.

"You better behave."

Patches nosed her pockets for the treats he knew lived there.

She'd given him a half hour of drills by the time Mrs. Johnson arrived.

"Sorry I'm late," she called from the railing around the covered ring. "You want me now?"

"Yes." DJ stopped Patches in front of her. "We'll keep to the far end of the ring." She watched Mrs. Johnson mount and settle herself in the Western saddle. "Now, remember, with Patches, you have to watch him every minute. He will test you every chance he gets."

"I know. Boy, do I know."

"Okay, let's see you walk, keeping fairly close to the rail. Walk on."

To DJ's relief, Patches obeyed the entire lesson. He laid his ears back when ordered to back up, but other than that, the lesson was all DJ could have asked for.

"I have a favor to ask. Since I have an appointment on Thursday, is there any chance you could fit me in tomorrow afternoon? I'll try to get things straightened out by next week."

DJ thought a moment. While it meant no riding time for her, other than her own lesson, she agreed. "Make sure you rub him down good. He works up a sweat trying to behave." She gave the horse a pat on the neck. "Good going."

Riding Major was like all good dreams rolled into one any time, but especially compared to Patches. DJ warmed her horse up slowly, still concerned about the leg he had injured in the landslide. But Major showed no sign of a limp and did all she asked with such willingness, she could have sent up skyrockets.

When she finished with him, her three girl students were lined up at the railing, waiting for her.

"He sure is smooth on the changes," Samantha called, flipping her long red braid back over her shoulder. "You've been working hard."

"We missed you," Krissie said when DJ stopped in front of them. "You okay now?"

"Pretty much." DJ ignored the twinges in her legs. How could muscles go so soft in only a week? "Sure hope you don't get the bug, Angie."

"Me too," the slender girl with big brown eyes replied. "Flu bugs and asthma don't mix too good."

DJ swung open the gate, Major backing up so smoothly she got a wink from Sam.

"The day Soda here does that, I'll bring chocolate chip cookies for everybody."

"Horses too?" Krissie nudged her horse through the gate.

"Yep."

The three gigglers moved off together, sitting relaxed at the walk but with their horses alert and ready to work.

The memory of Bridget's compliment regarding this class gave DJ the boost of energy she needed all of a sudden. If she'd been walking, her knees might have melted down. Instead, she slumped in the saddle, then rotated her shoulders. Sucking in a deep breath, she called, "Okay, move into a jog, slow and easy. Keep the pace around the corners."

She rode up by Angie. "More leg on the inside. Keep

him on the rail. Krissie! What's with your shoulders?" The blonde straightened her back immediately. "Good, Sam. Can you feel his mouth?

"Come on, all of you, deeper in the saddle. Just because you're riding Western doesn't mean you don't use your seat as an aid, too." All three had improved their backing skills since the last lesson. "Hey, did you know Bridget said you did really well?"

"Really?" The three girls exchanged surprised looks.

"She was tough," Krissie said with a wrinkled nose.

"It's good for you."

But as they filed out the open gate at the end of the lesson, Angie whispered, "We like you better."

By the time Joe dropped her and her bicycle at home, even DJ's teeth hurt.

The house smelled good, like pasta for dinner.

"Hurry up, DJ, we're about ready to sit down," her mother called from the dining room. "No, you boys sit here. DJ will be back in a minute."

DJ groaned her way up the stairs. She wanted dinner about as much as she wanted breakfast right now. She switched into a pair of sweats, stuffed her feet into her fuzzy slippers, and stopped off at the bathroom to wash her hands.

During grace, she nearly dropped her chin in her plate. Chewing the sourdough French bread took all the energy she owned.

"May I please be excused?" she said, her plate only half empty. The conversation had been going on around her, but for the life of her, she had no idea what had been said.

"Not yet. As I said, we will be having family devotions

every night after dinner." Robert smiled across the table at her.

"Oh." Anything more took too much effort. DJ stayed in her chair. They pushed their plates back, and Robert picked up his Bible.

DJ propped her chin on her hand and blinked a couple of times. Her eyelids wore fifty-pound weights.

"Tonight we will read from . . ."

DJ heard no more.

"Darla Jean, are you all right?" Lindy shook her daughter's shoulder.

"Huh?"

"You fell asleep at the table." She felt DJ's forehead. "You're not warm."

"Mom, Robert, I'm sorry. I can't remember when I've been this tired."

"You shouldn't have gone to the Academy. I knew it!" Lindy tipped up her daughter's chin. "Look at those eyes."

"Good night, DJ," Robert said. "Come on, fellas. We'll read a story, then you get a bath."

"Is DJ sick again?" one of them asked.

"If she isn't careful, she will be."

"Sorry," DJ muttered again, pushing back her chair. The stairs seemed fourteen stories tall. She never remembered hitting the bed.

In spite of a fuzzy head in the morning and the boys' constant questions, she remembered to take the drawing of Storm Clouds in to her art teacher.

"DJ, this is wonderful! You caught the imp in the foal, yet the tranquillity of the setting. Catching a feeling like this is difficult. You can be certain I am going to send this in to the competition."

One of the other students looked over the teacher's shoulder. "All right, that's excellent." Since seniors rarely said anything to freshmen, DJ blinked at him.

Any words that would have made some kind of sense fled. "Uh . . . uh . . ." *Kevin O'Conner, one of the nicest guys in this school, and that's all you can say? Come on, you can do better.* She swallowed and forced a "thanks" past a desert-dry throat. If her throat was as hot as her neck, she might break into flames any second.

"I'll make a copy and give this back to you. They said not to send the originals."

DJ stared at the cuticle of her right thumb. As soon as she heard Kevin move off, she dared to look up again. "Okay."

Mrs. Adams gave her a look that showed she understood. The flames heated up.

DJ fled to her stool and got out her still life. *Still life— that's me all right. Can't even be polite without swallowing my tongue.* After calling herself a couple more names, she took in a deep breath and let the air relax her shoulders. Tight as she was, she couldn't draw a curved line, let alone a straight one.

But the magic of pastels in her hands took her mind away from the boy wearing a red sweater sitting three rows behind her and over one stool. Soon she was lost in the drawing, in the coloring and the shading.

"You need to put your things away now," Mrs. Adams said.

The announcement caught DJ totally unaware. She blinked as if waking from a nap and closed her drawing pad. *The handle on that pitcher still isn't quite right,* she thought as she left the room.

This was one of the few times in her life DJ was grateful to see an empty driveway. The house would be quiet. But when she looked in the mirror, she was glad her mother wasn't there for another reason. One look at her daughter's white face and black-circled eyes and there would be no time at the Academy.

Maybe I ought to start wearing makeup, DJ thought as she changed into her work jeans and sweat shirt. *That would at least hide the circles*. She glanced toward the bed. If only she dared crawl into it for even fifteen minutes.

Instead, she slipped on her shoes and stopped at the refrigerator for an apple and a juice box, something new at their house. The boys liked juice boxes. DJ and Gran had been too ecologically conscious to want such things in the house.

At least they could recycle the soda cans.

She rolled her bike out of the garage and glanced up at the sky. Could rain, but then, maybe not. Ordering her legs and mind to get together, she pedaled down the street to Amy's and waved from the street.

Amy stuck her head out the door. "Gotta get my bike."

DJ leaned her forehead on her hands at the center of the handlebars. She'd never tried sleeping on a bike before. But now even that might help. *You'd think you'd be getting stronger, not weaker*, the inner voice taunted her.

"Hey, DJ, wake up. Time to go to work." Amy pedaled down the slanted drive and turned to head for the hill without stopping.

DJ pedaled after her. At the stop sign, just like yesterday, she had to pause for her breath to catch up with her. She'd left it somewhere around Amy's house.

Mrs. Johnson already had Patches out on the walker and was visiting with Bunny, otherwise known as Mrs. Lamond Ellsindorf, so DJ went on to Major's stall. During the short walk to the outside roof-only stalls, she played with the recurring questions about Bunny. Something about the woman bothered not only DJ but the other student workers, as well. No one could figure the newcomer out. Fit in she didn't.

DJ opened the web gate and entered Major's stall. "Clean already, boy. We got a good grandpa, huh?"

Major nodded and nosed her pockets for the treats. Ranger nickered, poking his nose over the highest bar, begging, too. She gave them each a carrot chunk, then using both brush-filled hands, gave Major a lightning-fast but thorough grooming. After brushing shavings out of his tail, she declared him ready for a ride. She and Major would have their own lesson—in jumping for a change—after her session with Mrs. Johnson.

"Feels like years since we jumped, doesn't it, fella?"

Major lipped another carrot off her palm and munched in her ear. She bent over and ran her hands down his front legs, feeling for the hot spot that had been there for so long now. Nothing.

"I'll tack him up now if you are ready for us." Mrs. Johnson and Patches stopped in the aisle.

"Sure enough." DJ straightened and gave the woman a quick smile. "Remember, it may still take some time to loosen him up."

"I'm not so concerned about loosening him up as calming him down. He's such a show-off." She dug in her pocket for a piece of horse cookie, Patches' favorite treat. As he munched, she stroked his nose, talking nonsense with him.

DJ smiled again. Women sure were suckers for their horses, herself included. In a couple of minutes, she headed for the arena, meeting Mrs. Johnson leading Patches. "If you want to mount up, I'll handle the gate."

"Thank you, dear. I wasn't going to attempt that yet."

"He's getting there. He just doesn't like to be rushed into new things. Takes his time getting used to them." DJ swung the gate open, and Patches backed away. "Keep a firm hand on those reins and use your legs. Once he knows for sure you plan on being the boss, he'll knock it off." DJ felt like crossing her fingers behind her back. She'd always shown him who was boss, and still he dumped her.

They moved to the end of the arena, and the pair began circling at a walk. Patches twitched his tail and laid back his ears once in a while but, other than that, shifted smoothly into a jog, then back to a walk.

When the other rider using the ring exited, DJ motioned Mrs. Johnson to use the entire ring. "Just keep him at an even jog on the rail. Take a deep breath in through your nose and out through your mouth and relax your lower back."

But at the far corner, Patches threw up his head. With one leap, he tore around the arena. Ears back, bit in his teeth, Patches looked to be running straight into the fence.

8

"TURN HIM INTO THE CENTER!"

Mrs. Johnson hauled on the reins, and Patches swung into circling the ring. All of the other riders moved their horses out of the ring to keep from being smashed into.

"The center. Rein him into the center!" DJ shouted to be heard but kept her voice even. Her heart felt like it was jumping out of her chest.

The whites of his eyes showing, Patches tore around the arena.

"Turn him into the center!"

Mrs. Johnson clung to the saddle horn with one hand. She pulled on the reins, but Patches ignored her.

Around again.

"Rein him tight into the center. Pull on the inside rein!" DJ could hear the other riders. When one said, "I'll go get her," she was grateful to hear another tell him no.

God, help her hear me. Calm her, please. Calm me! "Mrs. Johnson, rein Patches into the center of the arena!" DJ wanted to run to the rail and grab Patches' reins herself, but she knew she or Mrs. Johnson or all three of them could get hurt that way. *God, please keep her in the saddle.*

Patches circled the arena three times as DJ continued to call to his rider. Sweat dotted the horse's neck, foam flicked backward from his bit. He charged on.

"The inside rein. Turn him to the inside!" DJ felt like a broken record. When was that fool horse going to run out of steam? How long could he keep from running into the railings?

Mrs. Johnson let go of the saddle horn. She took the reins in both hands and pulled back on the inside rein as DJ ordered once again. Pulled into the tighter circle, Patches slowed. He came to a shuddering stop only three feet from DJ.

DJ grabbed the reins right under the horse's chin. She wanted to beat him over the head with anything she could pick up—maybe a two-by-four would get through his thick skull. Calling him every name she could think of in her mind, she looked up at the white-faced rider. "Why don't you relax now and get your breath?"

"Way to go, Mrs. J," one of the other riders called. "You just made it through every rider's nightmare."

"You showed him who's boss!"

At DJ's signal, the other riders moved off. She waited.

Mrs. Johnson still clung to the saddle horn. Her hands were shaking so badly she could hardly reach up to wipe away the tears.

"I . . . I'm s-s-sorry."

"You have nothing to be sorry for. The idiot here spooked at nothing and got away with it."

Patches stood, sides heaving, nostrils flared so they glowed red. He snorted, blowing snot and foam all over DJ's arm.

"Thanks, Patches, as if you haven't done enough." DJ talked to the horse, knowing Mrs. Johnson needed some time to recover.

Taking a deep breath, Mrs. Johnson straightened her back and patted Patches' neck. "If I *never* do that again, it will be too soon." She shook her head. "I let myself get in too much of a rush and didn't leave him on the hot walker as long as you suggested. This is all my own fault."

"But you learned something." DJ could hear Bridget's words coming out of her own mouth.

Mrs. Johnson nodded and sighed again. "Why do I always have to learn the hard way?"

Knowing she didn't expect an answer, DJ smiled. *How come I always learn that way, too?* She'd often asked Gran that same question.

"Well, I guess I better put him away for now." Mrs. Johnson gave DJ a look stuffed full of appeal.

DJ shook her head. "Nope, now we finish the lesson."

"You're kidding, right?"

DJ shook her head again. "Bridget's rules. Unless you are too broken to do so, you get back on and get over the fear right now."

"Why, it . . . it's not fear, it's just th-that I . . ." The woman stared at DJ. "You mean it, don't you?"

"Yup. Really, it's the best way." *What if she refuses?* Since this was DJ's first adult student, she tried to stay cool. If Mrs. Johnson said "no way," what could she do? Tell Bridget?

Shaking her head, the woman gathered her reins, shot DJ a dirty look, and shoved her foot in the stirrup. Patches never twitched a hair as she swung aboard. "What now, sergeant?"

DJ swallowed a grin. "You walk around the ring once, then I'll signal you to a jog. We'll just see how Patches behaves."

Patches played the part of model horse for the rest of the lesson.

DJ drew in a deep sigh of relief. What would she have done if . . .

"You did well, *ma petite,*" Bridget said from the railing after Mrs. Johnson took Patches back to the barn. "Level head, level voice. You kept everyone calm."

"Maybe on the outside, but my heart pounded so hard,

I couldn't hear myself talk. What if he'd crashed into the fence?"

"But he did not. Patches is no fool."

"Coulda fooled me."

Bridget let a smile flicker across her face. "I know he seems that way, but he just likes to get the upper hand. If Mrs. Johnson had done like you told her, this might not have happened. One thing, remind her to watch out for that place where Patches spooked. You can be sure he will remember and try it again."

"I felt like braining him."

"But feeling and doing are two different things, *non*?

DJ nodded. "Thanks for the compliment."

"You are very welcome. I will see you in a half hour in the outside ring, yes?"

DJ could feel a grin stretching her face at the same time as the tiredness drained out her toes. Jumping! She could finally jump with Major again. "I'll be ready."

Major wuffled in her ear as she dug the hoof-pick out of the bucket.

"Good thing you stay as clean as you do," she muttered while picking his hooves. Major nudged her seat and nearly knocked her over. "Good job, horse. Another one like that, and I'll tie you down." On the off front hoof, the shoe jiggled when she picked at it. Dirt had caked under it, making the job extra hard. "I'll call the farrier when I get home," she promised herself. *Wonder if he has time Saturday morning? That would be a miracle. Bet he's booked a week or more ahead.*

The inner monologue continued while she saddled Major, adjusted the bridle, and led him outside. As the shy sun kept ducking behind the western clouds, all she could think of was the dry weather. The ring was dry enough for jumping. She didn't need stirrups to mount with—she used her wings to fly up into the saddle.

"That sure was a circus out there this afternoon," Bunny said as she exited the outer ring. "I couldn't believe how calm and cool you stayed."

"Uh, thanks." DJ nodded and rode on in. *Where did that come from?* She looked over her shoulder to see the petite blonde riding her horse toward the barn. *Someone been feeding her nice pills or something?*

DJ took plenty of time to warm up Major, walking the ring, including the cavalletti bars, then trotting. Major kept his ears forward, snorting and almost dancing his pleasure.

"You're feeling mighty frisky, aren't you?"

The horse bobbed his head, as if he understood every word.

DJ leaned forward and stroked his neck, smoothing his mane to the right side. She wanted to wrap her arms around his neck and hug him. She had a sound horse again, her own horse, a willing animal who was becoming a better athlete all the time. The sun shone, turkey vultures crisscrossed the sky above the green hills, and the jumps awaited them.

Major danced sideways when a breeze twirled his tail and brought the fresh fragrance of growing grass and budding leaves. He snorted and played with the bit, adding his own notes to the music of coming spring. A cow bellowed down in the flat, and another answered. A horse whinnied from within the barns, echoed by one from the pasture.

DJ hummed a marching song as they pranced across the cavalletti. When she turned Major toward the first jump, she could feel his excitement. "You like jumping about as much as I do, huh?" They took them all like they'd practiced flying only moments before. When she went around the course again, they felt like one machine, oiled, smooth, and primed for power.

"One would think there had been no break for the two of you." Bridget shut the gate behind her as she called her greeting.

DJ finished the jumping course and rode into the middle, stopping right in front of her teacher. "I have missed this so much I can't tell you."

"I know, ma petite, you have been patient. But your dressage work is showing in the way you give your aids and the strength you are both gaining. Major bends around your leg now like he should, but you need to keep him more on the bit. Encourage him to bring the power from his rear, and he will become ever stronger."

DJ nodded. She, too, could feel the difference. "Thank you, Bridget, for insisting I work on dressage. I promise I won't argue anymore when you ask me to do something I'm not pumped to do."

"Did you argue?" One eyebrow cocked, and a smile twitched at the corners of Bridget's wide mouth.

DJ grinned back at her. *"Moi?"*

"Good, now I want you to go around again and concentrate on your legs. Drive him forward so he is all collected power. Then he will not expend so much energy on each jump and when the jumps are raised, he has energy enough in his reserves."

DJ nodded. "And has more to push off with."

"Precisely."

Before the hour was over, Bridget had raised the poles and caught DJ losing her concentration.

Fiddle, and here I was going for a perfect lesson. She concentrated on counting the strides between the jumps, mentally checking the placement of her legs and hands. Major touched the ground again so lightly she could have been a feather on his back. If ears could grin in delight, his did.

"That jump was as close to perfection as I've seen you do. Replay that in your mind often, exactly how it felt, what you did. Think about it right before you go to bed at night. Relive, replay the experience. Then when you are going to jump again, bring it all back."

DJ nodded. While she'd heard Bridget talk about re-playing and preplaying before, this time she understood it clear down to her toenails. *Replay what you do well, then preplay the experience again before jumping.* She repeated the words to herself to brand them on her memory.

"The more you do this, the more it will become second nature for you. Replay and preplay is a tool the Olympic winners use." Bridget laid her hand on DJ's knee. "Use it well. Now, go around again—and focus."

DJ and Major took the course at a perfectly collected, powerful gait, sailing over the three-foot jumps as if they were inches high. Major flicked his tail at the end and can-tered back up to Bridget. He extended his nose, as if to say, "You can congratulate me with a nose rub, if you like."

Bridget obliged, laughing up at DJ. "Your horse is as much of a character as you are. What a team."

"We should have had that run on video so you could watch it yourself." Bunny leaned her crossed arms on the top rail of the fence. "Then others could watch it, too, as a good training tool."

DJ hadn't even noticed they had a spectator. She waved toward Bunny with a surprised "Thanks."

"Make sure you cool him down well, now," Bridget said, raising her hand in a circled thumb and forefinger salute.

"I will. Thanks, Bridget. What a lesson!" She walked Major around the arena, paying close attention to any weakness in his front leg.

Bunny was waiting for them when they finally exited the arena. Several other riders had come out to try the jumps. The sun had disappeared behind the hills and with that, the temperature dropped.

DJ dismounted to walk Major back toward the barn.

"You've come a long way since the first time I watched you jump." Bunny fell into step beside her. "And the way you handled that runaway in the other arena. You are one cool young lady under pressure."

Is this the same woman who was yelling in the barn last week? How come she's being so nice to me?

When hasn't she been nice to you? The small voice inside her head asked. *Remember that time . . .*

DJ shut off the voice so she could pay attention to Bunny. "Thank you."

"I wish I'd had that kind of cool when I was your age. In fact, I wish I had it now."

DJ reminded her face to behave. Question marks all over it would not be *cool*.

"How did you get that way, or were you born patient?"

No matter how hard she tried, DJ couldn't hold back her snort at that comment. "That's not what my mother would say. Me either."

"Really? So where did it come from?"

DJ thought a moment, her eyes squinting a bit in the process. "I'd say what patience I do have came because of my grandmother's prayers and the way she's trained me. Bridget, too—on the training, that is."

"She's a great trainer. A better trainer than competitor, I think. That was the one saving grace of having to move to this area—I could work with Bridget Sommersby."

"You didn't want to come here?"

"Ha, are you kidding? My life was perfect before we moved here." Then, as if she'd said too much, Bunny moved off to another aisle. "See you later, DJ."

"What was that all about?" Amy asked when Major and DJ approached the stall.

DJ shrugged. "Got me. She sure was nice, though."

"She wants something." Amy petted Major's nose.

"Amy!"

"Doesn't she, Joe? You said the same thing."

"You guys are too suspicious." DJ led Major into his stall, and Joe began to strip off the saddle.

"Wish I'd been watching your lesson." Joe laid the saddle over the top of the lower door.

"How do you know about it?"

"Bridget." Amy handed DJ the grooming bucket.

"That lesson was the coolest, most awesome thing in my whole life." DJ's voice softened, like she'd been praying.

"Even better than seeing Stormy born?" Amy asked.

DJ tilted her head and thought a moment. "Maybe."

"You just have time to clean up," her mother said when DJ walked in the door later.

"DJ! DJ!" Bobby and Billy flung themselves at her legs.

DJ leaned down and hugged them both. She still felt like hugging the whole world. "So how'd school go?"

"We was sad. We won't go there anymore." The two ran their sentences together as if one person were speaking.

"But we had a party. Mommy brought cupcakes and juice."

DJ glanced up at her mother.

Lindy smiled back. "After all, it *was* their last day."

A tiny spear tried to penetrate DJ's heart, but she blinked it away. One thought made it through. *Since when does my mother do cupcakes?* She quickly looked back down at the boys. "Bet you had fun. Chocolate frosting, right?"

"How'd you know?" Both sets of eyes went round.

"I'm smart." DJ tapped her temple.

Two pairs of fists hit hips. The boys tipped their heads. Did some puppet master pull strings for both of them at the same moment?

DJ tickled one, then the other. "You've got frosting on your shirt, B."

They both looked at the spot on one boy's chest and broke out in giggles.

Robert appeared in the doorway. "Now, if this isn't a Kodak moment. Wish I had a camera."

The boys ran to him, telling him all that DJ said and did.

Robert looked at her over the boys' heads. His smile felt like a hug.

"You better hustle." Lindy waved a wooden spoon at DJ, then turned back to stirring something on the stove.

"I'm going." DJ bounded up the stairs. "Do I have time for a shower?" she called over her shoulder.

As her mother's "yes" floated up, DJ hit the bathroom at warp speed.

After dinner was finished and Robert was putting away the Bible from devotions, he said, "Can you have your chores done by 9:00 on Saturday morning, DJ?"

"Why?" DJ paused in the act of pushing back her chair.

" 'Cause we's going to the zoo!" the boys shouted.

DJ flashed a look at her mother.

Lindy nodded. "We thought since Robert can finally take a day off, we would do something as a family."

"Is that a problem?" Robert asked.

But I always spend Saturday at the Academy! While her mind screamed the words, DJ glanced from Robert to her smiling mother. So much for a perfect day.

9

"BUT I . . . I ALWAYS SPEND Saturday at the Academy."

"Are you teaching any lessons that day?" Robert asked.

DJ shook her head. "But I was hoping to get the farrier scheduled. Major has a loose shoe, and Bridget wants me to start work with a new horse and . . ."

"Did you set a time for that?" Robert laid a hand on Lindy's when she started to say something.

DJ wished she could tell a white lie and say yes, but Gran had taught her well God's opinion on liars. So she shook her head again.

"Then, how soon can you be ready to leave that morning?"

DJ knew how a mouse felt when the cat pounced.

"Don't you want to go to the zoo with us?" The boy on her right looked up with puppy dog eyes.

"No, I mean . . . that's not what I mean. I . . ."

"We want you to go." The little eyes on her left tore her heart in two. When the twins ganged up on her like that, she wanted to scream. She made the mistake of looking at her mother.

Lindy's eyebrows nearly met in the center, divided only by two deep, vertical slashes.

DJ knew her mother well enough to know that only Robert's hand on hers kept her silent and in her chair.

But Saturday is mine! I need time with Major, and I never get to be with my friends there anymore.

Silence—a silence that pressed against her eardrums like a thousand-decibel stereo on full force.

One of the boys sniffed and got off his chair, circling the table to stand next to his father. The other did the same, taking up a post by Lindy, who put her arm around him.

DJ felt like she was back on the wrong side of that very thick plate-glass window. And there was no rock in sight.

Resentment puckered her mouth like sucking a lemon.

How come I always have to give up my things? It's not fair! Another glance at her mother said that if she stormed out of the room, there would be serious repercussions. Like being grounded for time and eternity.

DJ gritted her teeth. "Can I have until 10:00 or 10:30?"

Robert nodded. "I think that can be worked out, if you can be ready to leave at 10:30."

"You said right after breakfast." The boys looked up at their father.

"This will be fine. You can go over to the house with me first."

"May I be excused?" Being polite took every bit of tooth enamel she owned.

"Do you have homework?" Lindy still didn't look very happy.

"When don't—" DJ checked her smart remark. "Yes." She picked up her plate and silverware.

"Of course you may be excused." Robert smiled at her. "Thanks, DJ."

Now she felt like a run-down boot heel. Why did he have to be so nice? She took her things into the kitchen, snagged a soda from the refrigerator, and headed up the stairs. After calling the farrier, who couldn't come until next Wednesday after all, she attacked the stack of books on her desk.

Every once in a while, she could hear laughter from the family room as the rest of the "family" watched a video. The glass between them doubled in thickness.

Later, the Double Bs knocked on her door. "We brought you some popcorn, DJ."

"Come on in."

Carefully, they set a big bowl of buttered popcorn on the corner of her desk. "We helped make it," said one. The other nodded.

"Thank you." She looked at them both through slightly squinted eyes. "You know what?" She popped several kernels in her mouth.

They shook their heads.

"I have to have a way to tell you apart. What is something different between you two?"

The boys shrugged, looking at each other with mirror faces. "I'm Bobby," said one.

"And Billy," the other. They looked at each other again. "Most times Daddy can't even tell us apart. So he guesses."

"Does he get it right?"

They nodded. "Sometimes."

"Maybe we should tattoo your initials on your foreheads."

Giggles bent them double.

"Oh, silly me, that wouldn't work, you are both BC!" She twitched her mouth from side to side and squinted her eyes. More giggles. *Well, at least I can make them laugh.* She shooed them with fluttering hand motions. "Get out of here so I can get my homework done. And thanks for the popcorn."

They giggled their way down the stairs, and DJ could hear them telling their dad about the tattoos. *Indelible marker would work awhile, anyway.* Her thoughts refused to go back to work. It wasn't as if she didn't like the zoo— she rarely got to go to the San Francisco Zoo, and she loved it all. But . . . would all her Saturdays be used for family things? And Sundays, too? How would she ever work it all in?

She clenched her teeth. Something had to give, and it wasn't always going to be her!

With that, she stuffed her mouth full of popcorn and slammed back into her algebra book. Starting a book burning entered her mind. Why was algebra so hard? Why did she have to take it, anyway? $Y=x$, how stupid. Who cared?

The boys came by later to say good-night, and sometime after that, Robert knocked at her door.

"Come in." DJ twisted from lying on her bed, where she was writing in her journal.

He stuck his head in the door. "Night, DJ. And thanks for being so gracious. From now on, we'll try to plan things further in advance so we can all get the things done we want and need to."

"Uh, thanks." Now she felt like a run-down and unglued heel.

But when her mother stopped by a few moments later, she came all the way into the room, shutting the door behind her.

DJ braced for what she knew was coming. The line had never disappeared from between her mother's eyebrows.

"I expect you to take part in family events." Lindy paced the length to the window and turned. "Without griping."

DJ bite her tongue. *Not fair! Not fair!*

"Is that understood?"

"Yes." DJ knew how to clip words, too. She'd learned from a master.

"Your horse is not—"

"His name is Major."

Lindy ignored the interruption. ". . . the most important part of your life."

Don't answer!

The silence pounded on DJ's eardrums.

"I expect a response."

DJ swung her feet to the floor. Would running help? She clenched her fists and clamped them against her thighs. "I—" she took a deep breath—"I know that. But I have responsibilities, too."

"Yes, you do, but playing all day at the Academy is not one of them."

"I'll be teaching another group again when the weather gets nicer."

"Perhaps not. We will have to discuss that. When Robert can take some time off, we need to be available."

Maybe you do, but I didn't marry him. DJ wisely kept that comment to herself. That silence again. How come silence could say so much?

"Do you understand?"

Mother, I am not an idiot. "Yes, I understand."

"Good night, then." Lindy made a motion as if to hug or kiss her daughter, but DJ crossed her arms over her chest and ducked away.

Lindy closed the door so carefully behind her that DJ knew she'd wanted to slam it. She thumped her fist on the pillow. She felt like opening the window and letting the heavy air escape. Instead, she crossed the room and looked outside, leaning her forehead against the cool glass. Word by word, she replayed the scene in her mind. True, she hadn't exploded like she used to, but why did she still feel like crying?

When she woke in the middle of the night, her throat hurt and her eyes burned. Had it been a dream? She'd been lost, and when she saw her mother in the crowd, she'd run right to her, but Lindy acted like she didn't see her daughter at all. She talked and laughed with whomever she'd been with. And walked away.

DJ went to the bathroom and blew her nose. Was she coming down with something again?

Saturday morning DJ tiptoed out of the house at dawn.

"How come you left so early?" Amy asked when she pedaled up to the barn much later. "I finally called your house, and you'd already left."

"I needed to get stuff done early."

"Great. I thought since it was nice, we could go riding up in Briones."

"I have to go to the zoo with *my family*."

"Uh-oh." Amy rubbed Major's nose. "Trouble, huh?" She cocked her head. "But you like the zoo."

"Not on Saturdays." DJ took the saddle off the door and swung it over Major's back.

"Robert being a pain?"

DJ shook her head. "My mother can—" She bit off the words. "But I didn't yell back."

Major nickered and looked down the aisle, his ears nearly touching at the tips.

Amy turned her head. "Joe's coming."

DJ opened the gate and led Major from the stall. "Let's

just say I have to be home, cleaned up, and ready to leave by 10:30. Patches is on the hot walker, and a note from Bridget said the owner of my new training job and her husband will be here to meet me at 9:45. They're moving their horse in then. If they're late, I won't be here. Just great, right?"

"Uh-oh." Joe patted Major's neck. "Looks like storm clouds here."

"You don't know the half of it." DJ shook her head and led Major toward the arena.

DJ worked Major through the dressage moves they'd been practicing but had no time to introduce anything new. She eyed the jumps, wishing they could repeat the day before, but she wisely stayed on the flat and over the cavalletti.

Mists rose in the open field north of the Academy and swirled around the bare oak branches before disappearing in the warming sun. A cow mooed from up in the park.

DJ stripped Major down, put him on the hot walker, and took Patches inside to tack up. She'd groomed him earlier.

"You were one smart horse," she told him at the end of the hour. "If you'd tried to dump me today, I think I'd have—"

"DJ, your people are here." Amy trotted up to the gelding's stall.

"Okay. Can you put him on the hot walker for me? I don't have time to cool him down."

"Sure."

DJ pulled off her riding gloves and stuffed them in her back pocket. She could see the dark blue horse trailer parked in front of the barn door. She glanced at her watch. She *had* to leave for home in ten minutes.

"Rhonda Samson, I want you to meet DJ Randall," Bridget said when DJ joined the trio by the trailer. "She will be training Omega for you, like I said."

"Glad to meet you," DJ said, her manners securely in place. She shook hands with a round ball of a woman who looked as if she could be bounced across the parking lot by any NBA player. Her smile and the twinkle in her turquoise eyes told DJ they could be friends from the get-go.

"She looks kind of young," Mr. Samson said to Bridget after greeting DJ.

"Age and ability do not always go together. DJ has turned two green broke horses into good riding partners, and I know she will do the same again."

"Well, if you say so." He turned to begin unlatching the trailer.

The woman shook her head. "Don't pay any attention to him, DJ. He wanted me to buy an old plug, thought it might be safer."

Her teasing tone made DJ even more certain Rhonda would be a great addition to the Academy. "So what did you get?"

"A three-year-old half-Arab, half-Quarter Horse filly. If I had the time, I'd train her myself, even though I haven't ridden for ten years."

"At least." The mustached man lowered the trailer ramp.

"Come on, Bob, you're just jealous because I didn't buy a Sea-Doo like you wanted."

Bridget and DJ exchanged raised eyebrow looks.

"So how much training has she had?"

"None, but she's been handled a lot so she is gentle."

It took all of DJ's willpower not to look at her watch. *Come on, I have to leave. You want me to be grounded for the rest of my life?*

Bob fussed with the tailgate a little more before Rhonda walked in and, untying the horse, backed a chestnut filly down the ramp. The horse picked up her feet like a balle-rina, almost dancing down the incline. Her coat glinted in the sun, even with the winter coarseness. A white blaze ran from her upper lip clear to her ears, disappearing under a thick forelock.

"She's a beauty," DJ said, walking around to check the other side.

"And smart as a whip." Rhonda stroked the horse's neck. "Won't take you long to get her in shape, I don't think. Meantime, I'll take English lessons from Bridget. I always rode Western before, but if you're going to have a dream come true, you might as well have it all."

Bob slammed the gate back in place and dusted off his hands. "I'll move the trailer while you take her to her stall." He glanced at his watch. "Then we gotta hit the road. I'm late already."

DJ checked her watch. "Oh, fiddle. Sorry I can't go with you, but I need to get home."

"I had hoped to see you   k with her a bit. . . ." Rhonda looked at her husband and made a face. "All right, I can tell when I'm being ganged up on."

"Sorry." DJ could hear her mother already. She turned and ran for her bike. At least she had taken a shower before she left home. She hoped washing would get rid of the horse smell or she'd get growled at for that, too. She threw her leg over the seat when the thought hit her. *Patches! Major!* They were both still on the hot walker.

She dropped her bike and headed back to the stalls. "Joe, could you please bring Major and Patches in from the hot walker? I'm late!"

"Sure 'nough, kid. You want a ride home?"

DJ shook her head. "I can ride it almost as fast as you can get the truck out. Thanks, I owe you one!" She called the last of the sentence over her shoulder as she jogged out of the aisle. She'd have gone at a dead run, but Bridget forbade running in the barns.

The twins were already in the car when DJ pedaled up the street.

10

DJ HIT THE KITCHEN DOOR at 10:29. "I'll hurry!" she said before her mother could get in a word. The look on Lindy's face already said more than DJ wanted to hear.

Robert shut the hatch on the Bronco as DJ charged out the front door. "Perfect timing, DJ. Did you bring a jacket? Could be cold over there."

DJ waved her fleece-lined Windbreaker. She climbed in the second seat, where the boys were already buckled in. "Hi, guys."

"We was waiting." The B closest to her handed her the left half of the seat belt. "You gotta buckle up."

"I know." DJ tousled the boy's hair, then clamped the belt in place. She could hear Robert and Lindy talking in low tones at the rear of the vehicle. *Come on, Mom, I wasn't that late. Lighten up. And besides, there was nothing I could do about it. You always said I have to be polite.* At the reminder of the reason she was late, she thought again of the filly Omega. She would be fun to break. The second thought wasn't nearly as pleasant. *How will I find time to do all of this?*

90

The boys fell asleep in the car on the way home, and DJ did the same not long after. The next words she heard were Robert's, "Let's just order in pizza."

DJ kept her eyes closed—opening them took more energy than she could dig up at the moment. They *had* had a good time. She could feel a grin coming on as she remembered lunch. She and the boys had been setting the hot dogs out on a round table with a blue umbrella while Robert went back for napkins and Lindy used the rest room.

DJ had turned away to look at something for one second when one of the twins let out a shriek. She turned back just in time to see a sea gull lift off with one of the hot dogs in his beak.

"He took my lunch!" The B flapped his arms at the bird.

Hearing the boy shriek, Robert charged back. "What happened?"

"The bird took my hot dog!" Bobby—or Billy—pointed to a circle of squawking and fighting sea gulls, one of which had the hot dog. Two others now squabbled over the bun. "Get it, Dad."

"I'll get you another one." Robert's laugh rang out. The boys looked at him, at DJ, who was trying to keep from hooting, over to the birds, and back.

"Bad birds!" the boys shouted together.

"You can have half of mine," the twin who had kept his hands over his lunch said.

"Here, you take mine, and I'll get another." Still laughing and watching the hot dog disappear down the bird's gullet, DJ handed her basket across the table.

"Thanks, DJ." Robert took some money from his wallet and handed it to her.

"Now, you guys hang on to your food." In a flash, both boys put their hands over their plates. "That's one smart bird." DJ shook her head, laughing her way over to the concession stand.

Even now, she could hardly keep from laughing. While her mother had missed all the action, she had thought it funny, too.

That evening after they'd devoured the pizza, DJ sat on the sofa with a boy tucked under each arm and read both *Horton Hears a Who* and *The Cat in the Hat*. They giggled at her different voices for the different animals and chanted some of the lines with her.

"Thank you, God, for my family," DJ whispered that night when she'd turned the light out. "And thank you for such a cool day." Those sea gulls, the boys shrieking, them all laughing—maybe this family thing wasn't going to be so bad after all.

Monday afternoon Bridget posted an announcement for a jumping clinic to be held at Wild Horse Ranch in the Napa Valley the first Saturday in April. Hilary Jones stopped right behind DJ as she studied the poster.

"Think you'll go?" the older girl asked.

"Sure want to. What about you?" DJ looked over her shoulder. "Hey, I like your hair that way."

Hilary wore her dark hair in dozens of thin braids, each ending in a row of colorful beads.

"Did you do it yourself?"

Hilary shook her head. "It takes hours at the beauty parlor. And, yes, I'm already registered. You notice who's teaching? Lendon Gray. I wouldn't miss seeing him for the world."

"Don't you ever have to ask if you can go to things like this?" DJ knew the poster hadn't been up the day before.

"Not really. My parents know how badly I want to become an internationally known rider. If we don't already have something important planned, I just write a check and register. I keep the important things in my calendar so I know what's going on."

"You have your own checking account?"

"Sure. I've had one for a couple of years now. My dad deposits my allowance in it, then I put in any money I earn. Dad said it was important for me to learn how to manage my money now 'cause one day I'm going to have a lot to manage."

DJ knew that money wasn't a problem in Hilary's family, but she didn't think they were that wealthy. "How so?"

"He really believes I'm going to make it into the big time. He's got my promotional campaign all worked out. Got my name on cereal boxes and all kinds of things. I'm not sure I believe all of that, but you've got to have a dream, like Bridget says."

DJ stuck her hands in her back jeans pockets. "I close my eyes, and I can see myself at the Olympics."

"Me too. We'll be on the team together, you just watch."

The flower of desire unfurled in DJ's heart region. "I want it so much." The words came out more as a prayer than just a thought.

Hilary stuck out her hand. "We'll make Bridget proud."

DJ took Hilary's hand, her skin golden against the mahogany of Hilary's, both hands strong with hard work and determination. The warm clasp made her think of them as more like sisters than friends. She looked up to read the same feeling in Hilary's dark eyes.

The moment hung, like a horse and rider in flight, held

up by air and determination alone.

"Together."

Hilary nodded. "Together."

Was that what the Apache had felt when they joined as blood brothers? The question played in DJ's mind on the way back to the barn. Gran called moments like these miracle moments. Couldn't times like that be a teeny peek into what God had in store for them?

Today she'd put Patches on the hot walker and start with Omega. What fun it would be to find out what kind of personality the filly had and if she was as smart and sweet as her owner said. DJ stopped in the tack room for a grooming bucket. She'd better get a move on or Andrew would be ready before she was.

Amy sat on the bench, her saddle beside her as she cleaned one saddle skirt. "How come these can get so dirty with a cover over them?" She dug her rag into the flat can of saddle soap.

"Got me. One good thing about riding English, the saddles have less leather to clean. Do you already have all your stalls done?"

Amy shook her head. "No wheelbarrow. One's got a flat tire, and Tony's using the other."

"Tony? He's cleaning more than just his horse's stall?"

"Yep, Tony. Guess he wanted or needed extra money, and now he's cleaning and grooming. Just like the rest of us poor slaves. Other than those who teach, like you know who."

"Yeah, as if I really miss mucking stalls. You can always do my saddle when you get done with yours."

"Your Crosby?"

"Get real. I'm only gonna use that in shows, other than enough to get used to it."

"But your dad said—"

"I know I'm supposed to use it, but would you?" DJ

shook her head. "Besides, if I left it here, it could sprout legs and walk off—you know that."

Amy sighed. "Yeah, Bunny says someone took a bridle of hers—it was even locked up."

DJ had started out the door but stopped. "Really?"

"That's what she said."

DJ swung the bucket, rattling the brushes and curry-comb. "Wow, nothing's been stolen around here in—" she paused, thinking—"in years. Stuff always turns up later, misplaced or whatever."

"I know." Amy used a clean rag to rub off the excess saddle soap and bring a fine luster to the leather. She lowered her voice. "What if she just wants to make trouble?"

"Huh?" DJ shook her head, making a face at the same time. "Why?"

Amy shrugged. "I'm clueless, but I think we better check with Joe."

DJ thought about the two very different conversations, one with Hilary that left her feeling like she was tap-dancing on top of a mountain, and the other with Amy that left a sour taste in her mouth and a confused mind. Why would anyone try to make trouble? And if the bridle was stolen, who would do such a thing? Had anyone told Bridget yet? The next meeting of the academy members wasn't until just before the jumping clinic up at Wild Horse Ranch.

"I sure hope this mystery is solved long before then," she said to Omega while she brushed the horse's back. "You stand for me to pick your hooves like you are for grooming and this job will be a piece of cake." The cross-tied horse flicked her ears, listening to everything DJ murmured.

She stood for the hoof cleaning, walked and trotted on the lead, and worked at the end of the lunge at both a walk and a trot.

"Someone's been teaching you well," DJ said when she returned Omega to her stall. She cross-tied the horse again and, after a pat on the shoulder, headed for the tack room to get a bridle and saddle. It was a shame Rhonda wasn't here to question about how far the filly's training had gone. Was she already accustomed to the saddle and bridle? Had anyone been on her back?

Obviously, the filly's training had not yet covered accepting the saddle. Her eyes rolled white when DJ tried to set the saddle on her back, and she pulled as far away as the cross-ties allowed.

"Okay, let's start again."

Later, Andrew was waiting by Patches' stall when DJ returned the horse to his stall.

"Hi, Andrew, what's up?"

"Bandit is ready for the lesson." The slender boy pushed back the lock of mousy hair that always fell over his forehead.

"Are you?" DJ removed Patches' halter and let herself out of the blue nylon web gate.

"I guess."

"Where's your helmet?"

Andrew fell into step beside her. "At Bandit's stall."

"You glad to be back riding?"

He shrugged.

Well, you're happier than you used to be. If only you liked to ride, you'd be the perfect size to sit on Omega's back once she gets used to the saddle. She tousled Andrew's hair, wishing she could give him an injection of her own love for horses. At least he was getting over his fear.

"You know, Andrew, I'm really proud of you for working hard at this. I know it hasn't been easy."

The look of gratitude in his eyes made her want to hug him. She still wondered how stories and footage on TV of a person falling off a horse and getting hurt could have such an effect on a child as they had on Andrew.

"Today we'll do review on the lunge line, then I'll walk

beside you while you ride Bandit by yourself."

Andrew came to a dead stop. His blue eyes had deepened in color, as if thunderclouds marred their surface. His chin squared, and he clenched his hands at his sides.

"It's okay. I won't be more than this far from his bridle." DJ held her hands about a foot apart. Andrew didn't say anything, but his eyes shouted *I'm scared!*

Bandit nickered as the two of them walked up. Andrew dug a piece of carrot from his pocket and palmed it for the pony. He didn't even flinch when the gray whiskers tickled the palm of his hand, or when Bandit nosed his arm, pleading for more.

"You want to bring him out?"

Andrew nodded. He unsnapped the cross-ties and led the pony into the aisle for DJ to check his grooming and tacking jobs.

DJ nodded and smiled at the boy. "Good for you. Bandit looks great." She tested the girth with two fingers. "Tight enough, too. Did he puff up his belly on you?"

Andrew nodded again, and this time a small smile tugged at the corners of his mouth.

"He likes to do that." She patted the pony's neck. "Okay, let's get to the ring."

"Where's the lunge line?" Andrew waited for an answer.

"Up at the tack room. Don't worry, I didn't forget."

Andrew did fine on the lesson until DJ unsnapped the lunge line. "No." Fear vibrated in that one word.

DJ paused. She knew it was time for this. Andrew *had* to become more independent. "I'll walk right beside his bridle." She forced herself to look into Andrew's eyes. "You'll be okay, I promise." She waited, thinking he might just dismount and leave the arena.

Instead, he stared back at her, as if looking deep into her heart to be sure she meant it. Then his shoulders drooped and he nodded.

DJ felt like she'd just kicked a puppy. "Okay, now, you know what to do." She waited.

Slowly, Andrew straightened his back, then his neck and head. He lowered his heels in the stirrups, took a deep breath, and evened his reins. Elbows in, shoulders square, he looked at DJ once more and nodded.

"Signal Bandit to go forward."

Andrew squeezed his legs and clucked the get-up sound. Bandit walked forward.

"Good job, Andrew." Together they circled the arena. "Now turn and let's go the other way."

Andrew tightened his inside rein, and Bandit obliged, circling toward the center and then back on the rail, walking the other way.

"Good. Now ask him to stop."

At each command, Bandit did as asked, even making a smaller circle, then reversing it.

With each accomplishment, DJ could feel the tension in the air relax and see the same with Andrew's riding. Back at the gate, she stopped after telling Andrew to do so. She turned back to face him.

"So how do you feel?"

An almost smile lightened the boy's eyes and nearly lifted the corners of his mouth. "Okay."

"Okay! Is that all? After your first ride by yourself?"

"You walked beside me."

"But you made Bandit do everything by yourself. Andrew, you did it!"

The grin made it this time. "I did, huh." He leaned forward and patted Bandit's shoulder. "Can I go now?"

"Sure. Lead Bandit back to the barn. I saw your mother waiting for you."

"You'll tell her I rode by myself?"

"You bet. I like giving people good news." She waited as Andrew dismounted and led Bandit through the gate, then

walked beside them back to the barn. While Andrew un-
tacked and brushed the pony, she told Mrs. Johnson how
the lesson had gone.

"I'm really proud of him," DJ said. "It wasn't easy, but
he kept on."

"I'm proud, too. He did better than his mother." Mrs.
Johnson lowered her voice. "I haven't told him Patches ran
away with me."

"Oh." What more could she say? She wouldn't tell Andrew, either, not until he was far more certain of himself.

"Thank you, DJ." Mrs. Johnson squeezed DJ's hand.
"See you on Thursday."

DJ headed for home, telling Amy all the good things
that had happened. "Now, if only Mom will let me register
for the jumping clinic."

"You got the money?"

"Yep, but not much extra. The farrier will be here
Wednesday." They both stopped their bikes at the end of
Amy's driveway. "Sure wish you were jumping Josh."

"I'd rather game him. Bridget suggested I start with the
barrels."

"Cool." DJ waved good-bye and pedaled up the street.
Now to ask.

But since dinner was about ready, she cleaned up first
and joined the others at the table. Once the food was served
and everyone eating, DJ took in a deep breath, sent up a
please, God, and dived in. "There's a jumping clinic the first
Saturday in April. Is it okay if I go?"

Robert looked up from cutting his chicken breast. "I
don't see why not."

DJ felt her heart leap. She could go!

Lindy looked first at DJ, then Robert. "Don't you think
we should discuss this first?"

DJ sighed. Of course it wouldn't be *that* easy.

11

"IS THERE ANY REASON DJ can't go?" Robert asked.

"I want to go," announced the boy on DJ's right.

"Me too," the other twin chimed in. As usual, DJ wished she could tell them apart.

"How about we finish dinner first and then talk about it?" Lindy said. The furrow appeared between her eyebrows as if by magic.

DJ groaned inside. Her mother could talk a topic to death. Why not just agree with Robert? And since when did they discuss things like this? The other voice in her mind answered the question almost before it was asked. This "discussing" was to be another "family" thing. Oh, for the simple days when she could just ask Gran.

DJ returned to the table discussion just in time to catch something about the boys' new school. Both Robert *and* Lindy had taken time off work to take the boys there for their first day. DJ tried to slam the lid on the little green-eyed monster peeking out of his lair. Jealousy sure was lurking. Since when did Lindy take time off work for *anything*?

DJ felt like she had two heads, complete with two sets of eyes and ears. One head paid attention at the table and the other meandered off. Maybe she was really two different people. One was here, and the other someplace else. She stayed with the one somewhere else. How was she going to get everything done at the barns? Four hours of teaching and working horses five days a week, plus one dressage and one jumping lesson a week with Bridget.

"Darla Jean!"

DJ returned to her at-the-table self with a thump. "Huh?"

"I asked if you had heard anything on the art competition?" Lindy's attempt at a smile didn't quite make it.

DJ could see the effort it cost. She shook her head. "No." She hadn't thought of it since giving the drawing to Mrs. Adams. "I won't be chosen. Remember what happened last time? Honorable mention. Big deal."

"Some people think honorable mentions are a very big deal."

"What's a horrible mens?" Bobby asked and Billy seconded.

DJ caught Robert's smile.

He turned to the boys. "An honorable mention is a prize for doing something very well, but not quite good enough for a fancy ribbon."

"Oh."

"DJ gets pretty ribbons at the horse shows."

"But not the art shows." DJ glanced at her mother.

"Yes, and that just shows where she puts most of her effort."

DJ kept her next comment to herself. Her mother just didn't get it. Horse shows counted. Art shows—well, they *were* better than algebra.

Thinking of which, she'd better get to her homework. She would ask again about the clinic after her mother played with the boys for a while.

"Can I be excused? I have homework to do."

"As soon as we have devotions." Robert reached for the

Bible he kept on a corner of the table.

DJ managed to keep a blank look on her face and the groan inside. A sneak peek at her watch said it was nearly eight already. And she had to help clear the table, too.

During the prayer, Robert asked God to bring healing to Maria so she could come back to live with them soon. DJ again got the idea she'd missed something else while she'd been off trying to figure out how to get everything done.

As soon as they said amen, DJ leaped to her feet and gathered up both her dishes and those of the boys. After a quick rinse, she loaded them into the dishwasher and returned for a second load. The others were still at the table, with Lindy pouring Robert another cup of coffee. DJ cleared the rest of the plates and silver.

"If you hand those things to the boys, they can carry them into the kitchen," Robert said with a smile.

DJ nodded. "That's okay," she said and kept going. Letting the boys help took even longer.

"No, I mean it. They have to help with chores, too."

DJ groaned. She handed one the bread basket and the other the meat platter. They followed her into the kitchen. "Just put them over there." One of the boys slid the meat platter onto the counter. A glass clinked over on the tile. Water spread across the surface and dripped down the crack beside the stove.

"Sorry."

"Yeah."

"I didn't mean to."

"I know." She could hear the jab of her answer. *Please let me hurry*.

She kept cleaning while he left the room, then hurried up the stairs to where her homework waited. She left the book report until last, and the clock had already clicked over ten by the time she opened the book.

At the same moment, she remembered the clinic. She still didn't have permission. She found Robert and Lindy dozing on the sofa, the late-evening newscaster talking about a shooting in Oakland. They both looked beat.

DJ paused. Maybe she'd ask in the morning. Just then Robert opened his eyes and, removing his arm from behind Lindy's shoulders, stretched and yawned.

Glancing at the TV, he said, "Is it that late already?"

DJ shifted from one foot to the other.

"What do you need, hon?"

"About the clinic." She glanced at her mother. "Did you . . . ah, I mean . . ."

"Yeah, we talked it over. You can go."

Lindy's eyelids fluttered open. "Go where?"

"DJ is asking for permission to attend the jumping clinic. I said yes. Any reason why not?"

Lindy looked up at DJ. "I think your attitude lately could stand some improvement."

DJ nodded. "Sorry." Now she sounded like the twins.

"I think all our attitudes could stand some adjusting," Robert said. "Mine especially. I think we're all feeling pushed. Having Maria back would make a big difference."

"But that won't be for another week or two, so for now we have to make do." Lindy swung her feet to the floor. "Thank God my mother and your dad will take the boys in the afternoons after school."

"I hate to impose on them like that but . . ." Robert shrugged. "For now, I don't see any other way."

DJ knew she should volunteer to help, but there was no way. "I can go, then?" This time she looked right at her mother. Lindy nodded. Before she could change her mind, DJ threw back a thanks and dashed up the stairs. She counted the money in her drawer. Not enough. She'd have to ask Joe to take her by the bank on her way home from school. Maybe she should just get a checking account like

Hilary's. Sure would make things easier.

The next afternoon, she took out enough money to pay for both the clinic and the farrier. Between training and shoeing, she was almost broke. Good thing payday was coming up on Friday at the Academy. Now, if only she could get the note cards reprinted and boxed and those portraits finished. But when? And how? Printing took money, too.

"Why the frown?" Joe asked when she swung the door to the truck closed.

"Just money problems." *And time problems and . . .* The little voice would have continued if she hadn't shut it off.

"Just, huh? You're kind of young to have money problems."

"You know what I mean."

"DJ, I don't know how many times Mel and I have said that we will pay for the clinics."

"I know, but Mom has a fit if I don't pay for Major's stuff on my own."

Joe nodded. He took in a breath and sighed it out.

She didn't quite catch what he muttered under his breath. Probably it was a good thing.

"How's the trainer doing with Ranger?" she asked to change the subject.

"Good. Of course, then he's got to train me. I think he's working with the smarter of the team right now."

"J-o-e!"

"Well, have *you* ever tried swinging a rope? Let alone roping a steer?"

"I didn't think cutting demanded that."

"It doesn't, but I want to learn the whole thing. Something about cutting and roping cattle that appeals to the cowboy in me." Joe parked the Explorer by the barn. "See you later. I gotta go home and get the boys. Gran has more work to do on that last painting. I groomed Major earlier today, so that should help."

"Thanks, GJ." She scooted across the seat to plant a kiss on his cheek. "You're awesome."

"We'll be by to get you later."

Later came too fast as far as DJ was concerned. Her dressage lesson started a half hour late because Bridget was in a closed-door session with Bunny and her husband. By the time she'd put Major away, Joe hustled her out to the truck.

"I know, I'm late."

"Gran has dinner ready. Robert got hung up at that new development he's started, and your mother is stuck in traffic on the Bay Bridge."

"And I fell off the jungle gym," one of the boys announced.

"Blood all over."

DJ turned and looked over her seat to the back, where the two were belted in. A white gauze bandage gleamed in the dim light on one forehead, right in the middle.

"See?" He leaned forward. "I got two stitches."

"Bobby?"

The boy shook his head. "Billy." His look accused her of not paying attention.

"I think you should wear the bandage all the time. That way I can tell you apart."

"I want a bandage, too." Bobby crossed his arms, and his chin jutted out.

Joe shook his head. "You two are something else." He backed up the truck and turned around to head out the drive. "Bobby, when we get home, I'll give you a dinosaur Band-aid, how's that?"

"I want one, too."

DJ leaned her head against the door window. This could get boring.

Joe had taken them all home and was reading a story to the boys in bed before Lindy slumped through the front door.

DJ could tell all was not okay by the sound of her mother's feet on the stairs. As if she took a nap between each step. She got up from her studying and opened her bedroom door.

"You all right, Mom?"

"I should be. I could have slept three hours on the bridge. Guess it was a four- or five-car pileup." She set her briefcase down. "Robert isn't home yet, either?"

"Nope. He said it might be after midnight. They had some kind of major problem."

Lindy rubbed her forehead. "DJ, I hate to ask this of you, but could you fix me a cup of soup or something? I've got to make another phone call, and I haven't eaten anything since noon."

"Sure. Chicken noodle okay?"

"Yes, fine. Are the boys asleep yet?"

"GJ is still with them." The two tiptoed to the boys' room. One of the twin beds held a sleeping ex-policeman beside a small boy, the other twin clutching a teddy bear as big as he was.

Lindy patted DJ's shoulder and entered the room quietly. DJ headed downstairs.

In a couple of minutes, Joe leaned against the kitchen doorframe. "I think I went to sleep before they did." He scrubbed a hand over his chin. "Guess I'll head on home. Maybe Mel is done with her painting and would like some tea."

"Thank you for taking care of the boys. I had so much to do." DJ poured the soup mix into the steaming pan of water.

"Did you get it all done?"

DJ shook her head. "If you mean caught up, I haven't been done with everything for as long as I can remember."

"That bad?"

Sighing out a huge breath, DJ shook her head again. "Worse."

Brad called Thursday night. "Any chance you can come up for the weekend?"

"Sure hope so. Mom's busy right now, but how about I ask her and call you back?"

"We sure would love to see you. Stormy is growing faster than any weed I ever saw."

"How about taking pictures?"

"It's a deal. For you, we'll document the growing of Stormy. Oh, and, Deej, Jackie said to ask if maybe we could try the horse show trip again. She has another competition, this time in Las Vegas. You'd need to miss only a day or two of school."

If you only knew. But she didn't say it. "I'll ask. It sounds like so much fun. Did you see the ads for the jumping clinic at Wild Horse?"

"No. You going?"

"I sent in my registration on Wednesday."

"I thought we had an agreement that I would pay for your schooling."

"I know, but Mom said—"

"Don't worry about it, kiddo. That's something your mother and I need to work out. Call me as soon as you know anything."

But when DJ asked, Lindy put the answer off until the next day. "I need to talk with Robert about it first. He said something about wanting all of us to go somewhere."

The last couple of evenings Robert had been working late and hadn't gotten home until sometime after DJ went to bed.

"But, Mom . . ."

Lindy shook her head. "I won't give you an answer, so don't get bent out of shape. Is your homework all done?"

DJ glared at her mother and returned to her bedroom. *As if she cares.* *"I've got to talk it over with Robert first. Robert wants to go somewhere."* "What about what I want to do?" she asked the face in the mirror. But there was no answer. She could have gotten a better one from the two little bodies now snoozing in their beds down the hall.

The next afternoon continued the downward spiral. When DJ looked at the grades listed on her report card, she felt like ripping it up. Now she'd probably never get to go to Brad's again.

12

"TWO Cs!"

"I got two As, too."

"PE and art don't count as solid subjects." Lindy looked over the top of the small folder of paper. "How could you get a C in language arts?"

"I . . . I didn't get another book report done, and I missed two papers. I thought I'd caught up after being sick, but I missed out on something."

"Sounds like more than 'something' to me. I can't believe you are being so irresponsible." Lindy raked a hand through her hair, the obedient strands falling back to where they belonged. "Didn't you check with your teacher after you were sick?"

Of course I did. What do you think I am—stupid? DJ clamped her lower lip between her teeth.

"All your grades count toward college now. You know that. And besides, this is about the worst report card you've ever brought home." She glared at the card again. "C minus in algebra. Not even a straight C."

DJ was careful not to mention she had been just three points above a D. "I *hate* algebra. Why do I have to take it, anyway? It's stupid, just like me!"

"Darla Jean." The words were a warning, the tone even more so.

"I can't help it! I'm doing my best!"

Are you? DJ wanted to put a cork in the mouth of her little voice. Or give it a boot wherever its behind was. *Why is everyone on my case all the time?* She wanted to grab the report card from her mother and run it through the garbage disposal—or bury it in the roses, but it probably wouldn't even make good fertilizer.

"If I thought you were doing your 'best,' I'd be glad for a card like this, but I know you have more potential than Cs."

Potential, smotential. "Well, maybe you're wrong!" DJ grabbed her backpack and headed for the stairs.

"Where are you going?"

"To do my algebra. I have a test tomorrow." *And the way it looks now, I might be taking algebra tests for the rest of my life. Besides, I don't understand what that . . . that teacher has been saying at all. He might as well be talking Swahili.* Only the fear of being grounded kept DJ from telling her mother what she thought of the whole thing. Did kids run away from home for reasons like this?

You could run away to Brad's. He's asked you, said you would always have a place to stay there. DJ paused in the midst of turning the handle on her bedroom door. Right now anywhere sounded better than here. She could hear the boys wrestling with their father in the family room. Their voices grated on her nerves like a dripping faucet. The house was never quiet anymore, at least not when she had time to be in it.

She shut her bedroom door with a minislam. The urge to kick it brought her foot back into kicking position, but she dropped her backpack on the chair instead. The sound of it bumping on the chair and then from chair to floor helped. Now they were going to tell her to come for dinner. *"Be polite while we eat. Take part in family devotions. Be nice to your brothers. Clear the table. Get your homework done. How come you still smell like horse?"*

"DJ, dinner's ready." Robert's voice floated up from the bottom of the stairs.

DJ glared down at her jeans. Sure enough, a smear from holding Major's foot to pick it decorated one thigh, and splashes of mud from walking the horses out to the hot walker dotted her legs. Not to mention the horse hair on her sweat shirt, including slobber, a gift from Omega. She sniffed her hands. Definitely horsey.

"I'm coming."

As soon as she slid into her chair, she saw her mother sniff, then stare at her. "Hi, guys," DJ said with a smile to each side. Billy now had a half-inch, very pink scar on his forehead. "Hey, Billy, how's school going?"

"Darla Jean—"

"Shall we say grace?" Robert interrupted her. They all joined hands. "Billy, your turn."

"Thank you for this food. Amen."

"That was sure quick," Robert said. He reached for the serving spoon. "Just pass your plates and I'll dish up the chicken and rice. It's too hot to pass."

DJ did as told, teasing first one boy and then the other in the process. When they both got the giggles, she half raised her eyelashes to check out her mother's face. Uh-oh, trouble for sure.

As DJ cleared the table, her mother said in a private-type voice, "I would suggest you don't come to the table like that ever again."

"Sorry, but there wasn't any time to clean up. Y—we spent my time talking about . . ." She'd wanted to say, "You were too busy yelling at me about my grades," but she didn't. She didn't dare look at Robert. She felt like a creep. A dirty creep at that.

"We want DJ to read us a story tonight," Billy announced.

"Sorry, I can't. Too much to do."

"How come you never have time to play with us anymore?" Bobby asked.

"DJ has homework. You will, too, when you get bigger."

"Yucky!" Dual voices.

The phone rang.

"I'll get it." DJ leaped for the receiver, glad for an excuse to get away from the discussion in the other room. "Hi, Brad. No, sorry, I haven't asked yet. I'll call you back in a minute."

DJ hung up and rolled her eyes. What timing!

"Mom . . ." She cleared her throat and said it louder. The others had settled together on the sofa.

Lindy looked up from the book in her lap. "Yes?"

"Ah, Brad is wondering if I can come up there for the weekend."

Lindy looked at her daughter. "How much homework do you have?"

DJ shrugged. "About the same as usual."

"Can you get it all done tonight?" Robert had an arm around each of the boys.

DJ thought a moment. "All but the book report."

Lindy shook her head. "I think you better stay home."

"But why?" *Why did I have to be so stupid about not changing clothes for dinner? That's what's bugging her.*

"Honey, why not let her go? Brad deserves a chance to see her, you know."

DJ sent him a thank-you glance.

Lindy sighed. "All right."

"Thanks, Mom, Robert." *Way to go.* DJ headed for the phone. *Should I ask about the horse show now? Brad needs to know.* She stopped and turned around. "One other thing."

"And so the big red dog—" Lindy looked up again.

"He wants to know if I can attend a horse show with

them in a couple of weeks. I'd have to miss school on Thursday and Friday."

Lindy shook her head. "Not with the grades you just brought home."

"But, Mom, it isn't like I flunked or anything."

"You heard me. The grades go up, and you might be able to do something like that. Right now, no."

"But that's not fair. I try. I do my homework and all the other stuff you tell me to do. I want to go with them." DJ totally ignored the voice inside that warned her to cool it or she wouldn't get to go for the weekend, either. "You're not being fair."

"Darla Jean Randall, you brought this on yourself. You know how I feel about good grades and working up to your potential."

"I would be if I didn't have to take algebra. I hate that stupid class."

"There will be all kinds of things you have to do in life, whether you want to or not. Besides, what about the other C?"

"That wasn't my fault. I thought I had all the homework caught up. The point is, you just never want me to do extra horse things. I could learn a lot at the show, but you don't care."

"Darla Jean," Robert warned, "that's enough. I won't have you talking to your mother that way."

DJ sent Robert a look that so plainly said "stay out of this" that even she took a step backward.

The boys started to whimper.

"Oh, for . . ." DJ glared at them. Both boys broke into tears.

"Darla Jean, now look what you've done." Lindy put her arms around the weeping twins. "There, now, it's okay."

"Sure, it's okay. They're not the ones who get yelled at all the time."

"Enough!" Robert's order cut through the angry air.

DJ started to say something else, but after one look at Robert's face, she decided not to. She spun around and headed for the stairs.

"You will not leave this room until you apologize to your mother, and to Bobby and Billy, too. You will not be going to Brad's this weekend."

DJ shook her head. "I . . ." Tears clogged her throat and burned behind her eyes.

"We're waiting."

"I'm sorry, all right?" Once again, DJ felt that thick glass drop between her and the four across the room. Their side was warm. Hers more like January in Siberia. She could see Robert's mouth moving, but the roaring in her ears garbled his words.

"No, it's not all right!" Lindy looked to be fighting tears, too.

"It's all I can do." DJ pounded up the stairs and into her room. She closed the door and leaned against it, fighting the tears that now clogged her entire head. What an idiot she was. If only she'd kept her mouth shut. *They hate me, I know it. This just isn't fair. No matter what I do, it isn't enough. Other parents are glad when their kids pass. My mother wants all As.* She threw herself down on the bed, pounding her fists into the spread.

"Darla Jean, you have a phone call." Icicles clinked on her mother's words outside the door.

DJ sniffed and, snagging a tissue, blew her nose. Sure, now she had to tell Brad she not only couldn't come to visit, she couldn't go to the show. If her mother had her way, she'd lock her daughter in her room to never do anything but school and homework.

Back down the stairs to an empty room. She walked the plank to the kitchen phone.

"Hello?"

"DJ, you didn't call me back."

"I know." She sniffed and blew her nose again.

"What's wrong?"

"Nothing."

"Right. Let's try that again. I'm not deaf, you know."

"I can't come tomorrow and I can't go to the show."

"You and your mom got in a fight?"

"Yes."

"Over coming up here?" His voice now wore an edge.

"Not really but . . ."

"But . . ."

"She, or rather Robert, said I could come up there, but then when I asked about the show, she said no." The words raced out.

"Help me here, Deej, I'm trying to understand."

"Just because I got two Cs on my report card, she climbed all over me."

"Ahh." The silence pinched.

"It's not my fault."

"Wait a minute. You say your grades are not your fault?" Now he sounded almost like Lindy.

"That's not what I meant. I . . ."

She could hear Brad sigh.

"Sorry about this, DJ, but you better get your grades up. I know Jackie will be really disappointed, too. Guess we better talk about responsibility one of these days. I'll call you later in the week." Even his voice sounded like it came from the other side of that thick glass.

She could hear Robert and her mother laughing with the boys in their room.

The cold wall followed her into her bedroom.

While she did her chores at the Academy, most of the

weekend was spent with her nose in her textbooks. She didn't even talk with Amy on the phone.

Monday afternoon when she walked into the art room, the teacher called her over to the desk. "DJ, you won! You were chosen to be one of the ten students for that weekend in San Francisco." Mrs. Adams bubbled in her excitement. "I knew you could do it."

DJ stopped in front of the teacher's desk. "You're kidding, right?"

"No. I mean it." Mrs. Adams handed DJ the letter. "Isn't it wonderful?"

DJ read the first paragraph. It did say her name all right. She glanced up at the teacher. "This is for real." Her body felt ten times lighter. She had won! Her drawing of Stormy had won. Wait till she told Gran.

"I told you so." The bell rang.

DJ read on. "April seventh!" She looked up and bit her lip. "I can't go on April seventh. I have a jumping clinic that day."

"Surely this is more important than a jumping clinic. Why, DJ, there were hundreds of entries, and your drawing was chosen as one of only ten."

"Sorry, I can't go." DJ handed the paper back. "I'm really sorry."

Mrs. Adams stared at her, her mouth slightly open. "But . . ."

DJ walked down the aisle to her seat. She set her backpack on the floor and herself on the stool. Keeping her eyes on the desk, she set out her drawing things and concentrated on the still life on a stand in the front of the room. Her stomach felt like it might leap out her throat. She'd told Mrs. Adams no, but what would her mother have to say about this?

GUILT MAKES YOU FEEL like dirt.

"DJ, what's up? You all right?" Amy stopped in front of Major's stall Thursday afternoon.

DJ looked up from picking Major's right front hoof. "Sort of." Amy hadn't ridden home from school with her today because of an orthodontist appointment. "What did the dentist say?"

"I have to have braces after all." Amy groaned and leaned on the stall door. "After all this time with that gross retainer. Yuck!"

"Bummer. Kids at school will call you tin grin for sure."

"*You* better not."

"Fence face?"

"Get real. Besides, you look like—uh-oh, you had a fight with your mom again."

"Not yet."

"Huh?"

"I haven't told her about winning the drawing contest." DJ set Major's foot down. She patted his shoulder and let him nuzzle her cheek. "That tickles."

"DJ, it's been two—no three—days. Are you going to?"

"I don't want to, but this not telling feels like lying and it's killing me."

"What's killing you?" Joe stopped beside Amy.

"Nothing."

"Oh, I get it. Something's wrong, and you don't want to tell your old grandpa."

"Sheesh." DJ reached for the bridle she'd hung on the door.

"Well, let me tell you that I always get the truth when I interrogate someone."

DJ rolled her eyes. "Double sheesh. How lucky I am to have a cop for a grandfather."

"An ex-cop, and don't try to get around me." Joe parked his rather large body in the middle of the stall door. Grinning down at Amy, he said with a wink, "Honestly, I don't think much can get around me."

"Doesn't look like it."

Joe turned to Amy. "So what's her problem?"

Amy shrugged. "Ask her. I've got work to do."

"Chicken!" DJ called after her friend.

"Well?" Joe waited.

DJ leaned into Major's neck and inhaled the fine aroma of horse. The scent reminded her of dinner last Friday when she hadn't changed clothes, which reminded her in turn of the fight afterward for which she had yet to really apologize, let alone ask forgiveness. The anger still simmered for not getting to go to Brad's or to the horse show. And all of this was because of that stupid algebra. If only she hadn't gotten a C in that the quarter before, too.

You were warned to bring that grade up. Besides, this time there were two Cs.

If that small voice that bugged her so was her conscience talking, she wanted to nail its door shut. The guilt it was building weighed heavier than a ton of alfalfa.

"So?"

DJ turned from both her horse and her inner war. "I don't have time to talk right now. I have to get out there for my lesson or I'll be late getting home again." She lifted the saddle and set it across Major's withers, grateful for the action. She knew that if she started telling Joe about the whole mess, she'd start to cry, and it would take too long. Bridget would have to come looking for her, and she didn't want that.

Joe stepped back but still blocked most of the doorway. "Okay. But only on the condition that if it's all right with your mother, you come for dinner with Gran and me tonight."

"So you can interrogate me?" She tried to make her comment a teasing joke, but it didn't come out right.

"If that's what it takes." Joe reached out and wrapped his arms around her when she turned to lead Major out of the stall.

DJ kept herself from leaning into the warmth and safety of his hug. "Thanks, GJ." The words barely made it past the rock in her throat.

The dressage lesson turned into a review, with Bridget working DJ over and over on keeping Major on the bit, no matter what gait or configuration she put them through. By the time they'd circled the ring both ways, turned, reversed, did figure eights, more circles, and the full arena with Bridget correcting every slip, DJ felt as if she'd climbed to a mountain top, dropped to the floor of the Grand Canyon, and been bounced by a bungee cord somewhere in between.

When Joe said Lindy had insisted DJ come home instead of eating dinner with Joe and Gran, she felt the bungee cord bounce her again. Now what?

Robert and Lindy were sitting in the family room when DJ walked in the front door. Something felt strange. DJ paused a moment. No noise. "Where are Bobby and Billy?"

"At Gran's." Lindy leaned back and crossed her arms.

"Sit down, DJ." Robert indicated Gran's old wing chair.

"I need to get washed up and—"

"Now."

It wasn't an invitation. DJ felt her heart thud clear down to her ankles. Something was wrong, big time. The urge to run up the stairs and lock herself in the bathroom nearly jerked her off her feet.

She crossed the football-field-sized room to the chair and sat down on the edge. Her feet wanted to run—anywhere but there. Why were Robert and her mother staring at her? Was that sorrow in their eyes? Had someone died? Or was someone about to? That someone being her, of course.

She tucked her hands under her thighs to keep from biting into her nails.

"Now, Darla Jean." Robert leaned forward and folded his hands together, his arms resting on his thighs. "Isn't there something you'd like to tell us?"

DJ darted a glance at her mother, but there was no help there. Lindy wore that if-it-were-up-to-me-I'd-give-her-away look. Robert looked about as friendly as a judge—dishing out a death verdict.

If only Gran were here. I wasn't lying, just not telling the whole truth. Or wasn't I telling any of it? The voice refused to be silenced. How could such a discussion be going on in her head when her vocal cords refused to cooperate?

"I . . . ah . . . I'm sorry for the way I've been acting lately?" She hadn't meant it to be a question.

"And?" Robert drilled her with a solemn gaze.

Thoughts scurried through DJ's head like rats in a maze.

"Let me help you out." Ice coated Lindy's words. "Today I received a call from Mrs. Adams."

DJ sank against the back of the chair. Maybe she could hide under the cushion.

"I . . . I was going to tell you." She studied a worn patch on the knee of her jeans.

"Oh really? When? After the art weekend was over?"

DJ caught the motion of Robert placing a hand on Lindy's leg.

"No."

"When?"

"I knew if I told you I'd said no to Mrs. Adams, you'd have a fit and yell at me, and I hate that."

"Did you ever for a moment think that maybe, just maybe, this art training could be more important than a jumping clinic?"

DJ shook her head. Her mother made "jumping clinic" sound like a dirty word. "Not to me it isn't." She started to stand up.

"Sit down." Again, Robert didn't offer an invitation.

Like a wild creature trapped in a corner, DJ attacked. "You just don't get it! I want to be an Olympic jumper. Nothing else is as important to me as training both me and my horse for that chance. Olympic contenders work all their lives to compete, and I'm doing the same. I'll earn the money to do it somehow—and I'll live wherever I have to." Her voice dropped. "I'll do whatever it takes. I don't care if you want to help me or not! That jumping clinic is one step in my training and *I* paid for it." She collapsed against the back of the chair. *Now I'm in about as deep as I can go.* She waited for her mother to scream back at her.

"And that justifies lying to me?"

"I didn't lie." DJ studied her bleeding cuticle. "I just didn't tell you."

"That's called a lie of omission," Robert said. "And it's still a lie."

DJ couldn't look him in the eye to see where he stood.

She could tell he was upset, in spite of his gentle tone.

"If you don't get your grades up and—"

"Honey," Robert continued in that same voice. "Remember, we—"

Lindy flung off his hand. "I thought you were on *my* side in this. If you can't help me, then stay out of it!"

"There are no *sides*. We are trying to work out a problem with *our* family, and you are not playing by the rules we set up."

Lindy leaped to her feet, pacing the room until she stopped in front of DJ. "Right now I am so angry and disappointed in you that I can't even think straight. You are grounded until your grades come up, and I want to see all of your tests. That means no phone, no Academy, no—"

"Mom, you can't do that!"

"I can, and I just did. You think about the consequences next time before you lie to me." She turned and left the room.

DJ felt like a bomb had just exploded and there were body pieces flying everywhere. Hers. She looked over at Robert, who wore a totally blank expression. His fingers were white where they clamped together.

"I'm sorry," DJ whispered the words, but they screamed in the silent room.

"So am I."

14

EACH BOOT FELT LIKE IT was made of concrete.

Halfway up the stairs, DJ's knees gave way, and she sat down on the step. Head in her hands, she let the last scene replay in her head. Preplay, replay, what difference did it make in times like this? How could she call Bridget to say she'd been grounded for the rest of her life? And all because DJ had a dream.

And her mother didn't like it.

She hates me. I know it.

DJ pulled herself up by the railing and lifted her one-ton foot again.

"I . . . I really blew it, didn't I?" The sound of her mother weeping caught at DJ's heart.

The murmur of Robert's voice was undecipherable.

Don't listen in—you know what Gran says. That pain-in-the-neck voice again. DJ started up again, then stopped. So what if she heard something bad. Things couldn't get much worse than they were now.

"R-Robert, I'm so scared."

Her mother admitting to being scared?! DJ leaned against the wall.

"Sh-she m-might decide to go live with Brad and Jackie." A hiccup broke the words.

DJ had to admit the thought had crossed her mind—especially now. Brad at least understood her love of horses and her dream to jump, and he'd already said he'd help. But he had also told her to get her grades up. And he hadn't called since.

"I know she hates me." A nose was blown, then silence.

"So go to her." Now Robert's voice came plainly.

DJ ignored her heavy feet and headed for her room. Being caught eavesdropping would not be cool, particularly tonight.

But her mother never came. DJ's anger simmered. When she laid a hand on her chest, she could feel it, hot just below the surface. "I'm not going to tell Bridget I can't come—let *her* do that." She paced the length of the room and back to the window. "I *have* to be at the Academy. Bridget depends on me. If I can't ride Major or take lessons, then I'll have to deal with it." She propped her elbows on the sill. "God, I always thought you were out there, ready to listen, but where are you now?"

Go talk to your mother. "No way, not a chance." More trips to the door and back. She dashed away some moisture from her eyes. "Don't you cry, either!"

Her algebra made about as much sense as the Egyptian letters she'd seen in a photo of a pyramid. She slammed the book shut, stuffed her homework in her backpack, and turned out the light. When she tried to pray, no words came. Only an overwhelming urge to cry again. *God's probably mad at me, too*, she thought. *He might as well be, since everyone else is.*

She turned over and pulled the pillow over her head.

A note from her mother in the morning said she could do her work at the Academy but not ride Major. Breathing a sigh of relief, DJ dashed out the door to ride to school with the Yamamotos. No one said good-bye to her, and no funny little boy hugged her legs. No one wished her a good day. The boys were still at Gran's, and Robert and Lindy had left before she did.

"Uh-oh," Amy said after one look at DJ's face. "You want to talk about it?"

DJ shook her head. "It's too complicated. But I almost got grounded for the rest of my life." She sank against the back of the seat. "I can't ride Major."

"They found out about the art weekend?"

"Mrs. Adams called and talked to my mother."

"Yikes." Amy shuddered.

"You can say 'I told you so' any time now."

"I won't."

DJ shook her head. "I just wish she'd ground me from algebra."

She was beginning to feel better until she walked into the art room. Mrs. Adams shook her head when she saw her.

"I can only keep that spot open a few more days," she said. "I sure hope you change your mind."

My mother strikes again! DJ took her seat but her fingers failed to draw the lines the way they should. Another problem to deal with! "Fiddle. Double and triple fiddle!" She kept the mutter low.

After her work at the Academy, DJ flung herself into a chair at Gran's. "It's not fair!" She could hear her voice rising on telling Gran and Joe all about the problems.

"No one ever said life would be fair." Gran stopped behind DJ and massaged her shoulders. "God said He'd rescue us from trouble, and Jesus said He would always be with us, but no one said anything about fair."

"How come my mother can't be happy about me wanting to become such a super thing as an international jumper? It's not like I'm doing drugs or something."

"I don't know. Have you prayed about it?"

"I tried. I think God's gone shopping or something. He sure isn't answering."

Gran dropped a kiss on DJ's head and wrapped her arms around her granddaughter. "Oh, darlin', God never checks out. He is the same, yesterday, today, and always. He hears you."

"Then He's probably mad at me, too." DJ rested in her grandmother's arms. "Even Major hates me 'cause I didn't ride him today. This isn't fair to him, either." She turned to look at Joe. "That reminds me, I overheard Bunny saying something to Tony that made him boiling mad. I didn't catch what." She watched Joe sipping his coffee on the other side of the table. "Did you ever find out anything about her?" It was a relief to change the subject.

He shook his head. "Like I told you, she's clean as a whistle. You kids are seeing shadows where there are none. I think you've been reading too many mysteries."

DJ slunk back in her chair. "Not me. I'm two book reports behind. Who's got time to read?"

"But you used to like to read." Gran tipped DJ's chin up with one loving finger and brushed the hair back, looking deep into DJ's eyes. "Child, you need to go to your mother and, together, clear this all up."

DJ could feel her neck tighten. "Yeah, right." She knew that answer wasn't what Gran wanted to hear. "I wish I'd never shown that drawing to Mrs. Adams. That's what brought on all of this. I'm never doing such a lame-brained thing again."

"You think God made a mistake giving you a talent for drawing and a love of art?"

DJ couldn't think of a thing to say to that.

"So what are you going to do?" Joe broke the extended silence.

"Nothing—oh, I don't know. Get my grades back up." She turned to Gran. "I know I should go talk to her but . . . Gran, she won't listen. I think one thing, and she thinks another. That's all there is to it!"

Joe glanced up at the clock above the sink. "I better go get the boys. Robert took them to the new house with him so they could play there since Lindy won't be home till late. Have you talked with him?"

Again, DJ shook her head. "I really don't want to talk to anybody."

"So we're nobodies?" Joe wiggled his eyebrows.

"You know what I mean."

"I do, but you know what? Asking for help is not a sin." Joe stood up. "Do you want to come with me? I'll bring the boys back here, and you and Robert can do some talking. Trust me, my son listens well. I should know—I trained him."

"Is he an interrogator, too?" DJ almost pulled off the joke. Almost but not quite.

"So . . . you coming?" Joe waited at the door.

DJ shook her head. "I'll just have to try harder, that's all. Mom said I'm not doing my best, so guess I better." She shook her head again. "Things used to be a lot simpler."

Later that night, DJ tried praying again. "Please, God, help me get along better with my mother. And somehow I have to learn to understand algebra. How come I have so much trouble?" DJ yawned wide and waited, hoping for some kind of an answer. "You know that verse Gran gave me for biting my fingernails, 'I can do all things through

Christ who strengthens me'? It doesn't seem to be working."

How come God could seem so close at times, and others, like right now—where was He? The thought bugged DJ even as she fell asleep.

The birds started their morning chorus about the time DJ woke up. She dressed quickly in the dimness and tiptoed down the stairs. Even though she couldn't ride him, this way she would have extra time with Major, and she could work both Patches and Omega longer.

"Do you want a ride to the Academy?" Robert leaned against the counter, a steaming cup of coffee in his hand.

"Yi! You scared me." DJ could feel her heart thudding. "I though everyone was still in bed."

"Your mother's still sleeping. She needs some extra rest after the week she put in. And the boys will sleep until cartoons at least. They promised to be really quiet. I thought I could work on the house for a while, then come home for breakfast."

"I was going to ride my bike."

"Well, since I go right by the Academy, I'll drop you off and pick you up. If you want me to, that is."

"Sure." DJ dug an apple out of the refrigerator and a food bar from the cupboard. "I'm ready when you are." *So, do I talk with Robert?* She could hear Joe's suggestion as clearly as if he were right next to her ear. *But what do I say? "Hey, Robert, you have a dumb kid on your hands. I can't even do algebra."*

By the time she'd figured out what to say, they were driving into the parking lot at the Academy. "Thanks for the ride."

"Okay. See you in about three hours? Lindy said she'd

have breakfast ready at 9:00."

"I might just stay here, okay?"

"As I said, breakfast is at nine."

DJ nodded and shut the truck door. She'd bike back over after breakfast.

First she fed both Major and Ranger, shoveling the dirty shavings out as they ate. "You boys ready for a good grooming?"

Major looked over his shoulder and shifted to the side to make her work easier. He slobbered grain and kept chewing, rippling his skin where she tickled his flank. By the time he'd cleaned out his grain bucket, she had dumped in a wheelbarrow of shavings and spread them. All the time she brushed and curried him, they carried on a conversation. She explained to him what a mess she was in, and he nodded, snorted, and flicked his ears back and forth, as if understanding every word.

"You know what?" She rubbed his face down with a clean cloth after using a soft brush. "You're a great listener. Now, if only you had some answers."

DJ leaned against his neck. "And if only I could ride you." The thought of the jumping and flat work she was missing made the burn in her belly ignite again. How would she ever get her algebra grade up so she could ride? A week, she could handle. Two weeks . . . but until her grade came up? It might snow in July in San Francisco before that happened.

15

"WHAT DO YOU MEAN, you agreed to exercise Bunny's horse? Don't you have enough to do?" Lindy set the plate of bacon down with a clatter. The coffee cake she'd made for breakfast steamed in the middle of the table, and a bowl of scrambled eggs sat at Robert's right hand. Until just this very minute, things had been going almost normally.

DJ groaned. *Why, oh why, did I even bring it up?* "It's only for a week. And besides, I need the money."

"Back to money again." Robert pulled out Lindy's chair for her. He made a T with his hands. "Time out. I'm calling a truce before this goes any further. Come on, boys, let's say grace. Bobby, it's your turn." He held out his hands, and they formed the prayer circle.

"Bless Mommy and Daddy and DJ and Billy and me. Bless Grandpa and Grandma and our new house and Uncle Andy and . . ."

DJ stifled a groan. The food could be cold before Bobby ran out of blessings.

". . . and the good food Mommy made us for breakfast." When they all said amen, DJ glanced at Robert, who rolled his eyes at her.

"This is Gran's coffee cake. You made it?" DJ looked across at her mother in surprise.

"I can cook, you know." Lindy dished scrambled eggs onto her plate. "Mom and I used to make this breakfast when you were little like the boys and Dad was still alive. The coffee cake was your favorite, mostly because it was Dad's favorite."

"I hardly remember him." DJ held the bacon while each boy took two slices.

The Double Bs quickly took over the conversation, leaving DJ to eat in peace.

"Daddy, we going to see the new house?" Billy asked.

"Right after breakfast."

DJ brought her attention from training Omega back to the table. She looked across at Robert.

He smiled back. "I thought we'd all go look at the house. The interior designer has some questions she'd like answered."

"Can't I go another time?" *Whoops, wrong thing to say.* The look on her mother's face made DJ reframe her comment. "If I can be excused, I'll be ready in a couple of minutes." She could feel her mother's glare drilling holes into her shirt as she left the room.

"Hurry, DJ!" The boys nearly ran over her on her way up the stairs. "We gotta wash so we can go."

At the new house, Robert opened the front door and ushered them inside. "I think we'll start upstairs—"

"With the boys' room," the twins chimed.

"You can at least *act* pleased!" Lindy hissed directly into DJ's ear after Robert had shown them DJ's room with the Jacuzzi tub. Robert and the boys had gone downstairs ahead of them.

"I said thanks."

"Your gratitude leaves a *lot* to be desired." Lindy strode

down the stairs at Robert's call.

No matter what I do, it's not good enough for her. DJ followed the others, hearing the boys calling and laughing at each new thing. They jumped down the stairs into the sunken living room and ran back up the stairs to their bedroom next to a big playroom. Robert had told them about the places for games and a railroad track and playhouse fort. They laughed and shouted, falling down on the thick carpet and calling to DJ to come play.

"Later, guys."

DJ felt overwhelmed by her room. It was everything she could dream of, but the questions the designer asked were beyond her. What color did she want? Could she please choose some wallpaper she liked for the bathroom? Did she want vertical blinds or horizontal? Sheesh. DJ would rather clean out horse stalls. At least she knew what looked good there.

And her mother thought she didn't appreciate it. That wasn't it at all. How would DJ ever live up to such a great room?

"Can you drop me off at the Academy on the way home?" DJ asked when they were back in the car.

"No, I think it's time the three of us have a good long talk." Robert glanced at Lindy, who nodded back. "You can go over after that."

"Maybe." Lindy's one word set DJ's teeth on edge. *Are they going to take this Saturday away from me, too?*

Back home with the boys watching a video, Robert herded both Lindy and DJ into the dining room. "Okay, let's talk."

DJ wanted nothing more than to head for the Academy.

She'd rather talk with Major any day. He, at least, understood her.

Once they were seated, Robert turned to DJ. "Now, why did you take on more to do when you are already busier than two normal people?"

"Well, Bunny asked me if I would exercise her jumper for a week while she goes back to the East Coast. I said she should ask Hilary or Tony since they are such good jumpers, but she insisted I do it. So I said yes. He'd be fun to ride, kind of like riding Herndon. Besides, she's going to pay me twice what I earn for lessons." She looked toward her mother. "It's only for a week, and since I can't ride Major, I thought—"

"I thought that time was to be spent on your algebra."

DJ flinched. "Look, no matter how much time I spend on that garbage, I'll never understand it. I hate algebra, and I didn't want to take it in the first place."

"Watch your attitude."

"Yes, ma'am."

"You need upper-level math classes to get into college. You have to fulfill the entrance requirements."

"But what if I—"

"Do you really need money that badly?" Robert interrupted.

DJ nodded. "I just got Major shod, and he needs a new show blanket, plus worming and extra feed as we work toward another show. All that and the show fees and stuff you forget you need. Horses are really expensive."

"Which is why you have to have some kind of training to support yourself. Your artistic ability might be able to do that once you get through college."

"Mom, I'm in the ninth grade. I'm not ready to choose a college yet." DJ spoke through gritted teeth. *And besides, who says I want to go to college at all?*

"What happened to the money from your card sales and the portraits?" Lindy asked.

DJ flinched again. "I . . . I haven't finished all the portraits. I have two to go, and one lady is getting upset at the wait." She lowered her voice, mumbling the words, hoping her mother and Robert would drop the subject. "I was planning on doing them this afternoon. If I can ever get back over to the Academy."

"So your grades are slipping, the work you agreed to do isn't finished, and you've turned down the honors art class."

DJ half rose from her chair. "But I almost never miss school, and most of my grades are okay. I never claimed to be a brain. I teach riding five afternoons a week, train two horses for other people, and train and support my own horse."

"And what's more important?" Lindy straight-armed the table so the two stood nose to nose.

"To you or to me?"

"Okay, let's cool off again." Robert slapped his hands flat on the table.

DJ slumped back down in her chair, arms locked over her chest and one ankle resting on the opposite knee. She studied the seam on the inside of her jeans. *And this isn't helping. You're wasting my valuable time.* She glanced at her watch without appearing to. If only she dared to just leave the room.

"Can I go now?"

Robert shook his head. "How about if I help you with your algebra?"

"Dear, you're so busy now, you—"

"I know, but this is more important. I'll work it out somehow."

"It'd only waste your time." *And mine.*

"Let me be the judge of that."

"Whatever." DJ sneaked a peek at her mother. Lindy didn't look to be any more of a believer in this scheme than her daughter.

At the Academy later that afternoon, DJ and Amy pulled a hay bale into the sunshine at the front door and sat down to clean tack. "Robert's going to help me with algebra."

"That's cool."

"What a waste."

"Darla Jean Randall, if you'd quit thinking and talking like you can't—you know Bridget doesn't allow that word around here. If you'd think 'I can' like you do with everything else, you could even do algebra."

"Yeah, right, and pigs can fly."

"Don't be so pigheaded stubborn. You know I'm right." Amy thumped DJ on the leg. "If I can put up with braces, you can do algebra."

Was she just being pigheaded like Amy said?

That evening after the algebra session with Robert, she stood in front of the mirror in the bathroom. "I can do algebra." She repeated the phrase three more times for good measure, then went to her desk and wrote ten times, *I can do algebra*. In big, bold letters, she added: *I, DJ Randall, will never use "I can't" around algebra again!* She signed her name with a flourish.

Between muttering "I can do all things through Christ who strengthens me" and "I can do algebra," DJ caught the twins watching her with funny expressions on their faces. *They think I'm going nutsy. I probably am!*

"Bridget, do you have a couple of minutes?" DJ stopped in the doorway of the academy office Tuesday afternoon.

Bridget looked up from her paper work and, with a smile, pushed her glasses up on her forehead. "Of course. You do not look happy. How can I help you?"

If only you knew. DJ stopped in front of the paper-stacked desk. "It's about Patches and Mrs. Johnson."

Bridget nodded for her to go on.

"I think Patches is just too much horse for her right now. He needs an experienced rider, someone who can make him mind and not be bullied by him. Every time she shifts her concentration, he—"

Bridget nodded. "I know, he takes off or tries to dump his rider."

"And sometimes succeeds." DJ knew Bridget could enjoy the joke since the only other person whom Patches had dumped was DJ herself.

"This is truly a hard situation." Bridget rose from her chair and paced the floor. "You think she should sell him?"

"Yes. Before she gets hurt."

"She is not a bad rider."

"I know, but she would enjoy riding more if she could trust her horse."

"She did all right with the school horse."

"See."

"When is her next lesson with Patches?"

DJ glanced at her watch. "In a half hour."

"I will talk with her after the lesson. Is there anything else?"

DJ nodded. "I'd like to try Andrew with the girls' class. I think he'll have more fun there. He already knows them, and they cheer him on."

"Good idea. You want to tell his mother today?"

DJ left the office and headed for the barn. Omega would be cooled off enough to put away now. She sure hoped Mrs. Johnson had put Patches on the hot walker like she was supposed to. He wasn't out there when DJ had clipped Omega on.

Patches acted as if he'd never misbehaved a day in his entire life. He did everything Mrs. Johnson asked of him and acted as if he were having a good time, too.

He kept on the rail, for once not trying to rub off his rider on it. He changed gaits without an extra step and jogged along like he'd been doing it for years. DJ breathed a sigh of relief. Maybe she'd been wrong about him and spoken to Bridget too soon.

"Go ahead with a figure eight now, keeping that lope at the same speed. I want you to signal him to change leads at the apex of the eight so he goes into the circle on the inside lead." She looked up at Mrs. Johnson, who nodded with a smile.

"He is behaving so well today. You must have been feeding him 'nice' pills."

"Believe me, if I had such a thing, he'd have been getting them all along." DJ stroked Patches' nose. "Huh, fella?" Patches rubbed his forehead against her black sweat shirt, leaving white hairs from his star behind. "Okay, there you go, now."

The first figure eight went almost perfectly, with Patches missing the lead changes by only a stride or two.

"Be more definite in your aids, leg especially."

Mrs. Johnson nodded, concentrating on her horse.

Suddenly, out of the corner of her eye, DJ saw a flash of white. A white cat streaked across the arena, dodging horse hooves.

Patches reared and hit the ground at a dead run. At the fence he swerved, a hard right, leaving Mrs. Johnson to catapult straight into the lower railing.

16

"DON'T MOVE HER." Joe knelt beside the unconscious woman.

"What happened?" Mrs. Johnson blinked her eyes and moved one hand.

"Patches threw you, and you hit the aluminum rail." Joe's voice came slow and gentle.

It's all my fault. I should have ended the lesson sooner. DJ knelt on the other side, holding Mrs. Johnson's hand when the woman grasped hers.

"Your eyes look okay. Do you hurt in any one spot more than another?"

"My right arm. I think it's broken. I can't move my fingers." When Joe touched it, the woman groaned.

"We better call 9–1–1," Bridget said softly.

DJ didn't realize she was even there.

"No, don't be silly. For a broken arm?" Mrs. Johnson shook her head. "Hey, I've been a nurse for ten years, folks. I am not going into that hospital in an ambulance for a broken arm." She gave Joe a pleading look. "I would know if I were broken somewhere else." She extended her left hand. "Help me sit up, and we'll use my jacket as a sling. Do you think you could drive me to either emergency or urgent care?"

"Sure, but . . ."

"Look, Joe, I know you have first-aid training. I'm not bleeding anywhere, and while I have a bit of a headache, it's nothing like a concussion. My legs work, my mind is clear—come on, give me a break."

"Patches already did that," Joe said with a straight face.

"Great, you're even a comedian."

"You want me to put him away?" Tony led Patches back to the group by the railing. "It wasn't his fault, really. It was that white cat. The other horses spooked, too."

"I saw it at the same moment Patches did. Not quick enough to grab the saddle horn." Mrs. Johnson grimaced and turned white around the mouth when Joe and DJ helped her sit up. She cupped her other hand around the injured forearm. "DJ, could you please get me a bag of ice? The more we can keep the swelling down, the easier it will be to set."

"Sure." DJ started to leave, but Joe stopped her. "Bring several small bags so we can pack them all around the arm."

When DJ returned, Joe took off his jacket and fashioned it into a sling before he helped Mrs. Johnson to her feet. "This is silly. You lean against the fence while I go get the truck. Bridget, do you have any aspirin in your first-aid kit? Or something stronger. That will help ease the trip in."

"This is not your fault, DJ," Bridget said as the Explorer, carrying Mrs. Johnson in the front seat, drove out of the arena.

"My head agrees with you, but my heart says I should have been prepared."

"These things happen. Some horses just spook more easily. As you said, Patches is one of those. I will talk with her about selling him and getting something more dependable when she is better."

DJ was still shaking when she got home.

"Hurry, DJ. We have the boys' open house at school right after dinner." Lindy turned from the oven and sat a casserole on the counter.

"Do I have to go?"

"No, not unless you want to."

Robert even cut devotions short and, with the boys at full volume and speed, left the house.

The silence felt as drained of energy and sound as DJ did. She called Joe to find out how Mrs. Johnson was. He said it was a simple fracture. They set the arm, put a cast on it, and he dropped her off at her house.

"Andrew asked a lot of questions," Joe continued. "You have him in class tomorrow, right?"

"How will he get there? She usually brings him. She can't drive yet, can she?"

"No, but Mr. Johnson said he would take a couple of days off work to make it easier for her. When I left, she was tucked up on the sofa, grumbling about being such a baby. As they say, nurses and doctors make the worst patients."

"I should have—"

"Darla Jean Randall, if I hear one more 'I should have' out of you, I'm going to personally tape your mouth shut."

"Joe Crowder!" DJ heard Gran say in the background.

DJ couldn't help but giggle. Gran sounded horrified.

"Hey, kid, there was nothing anyone could have done, other than keep that cat in the house."

"I think it was Bridget's cat."

"Well, there you have it. I'll go yell at Bridget about how to take care of her livestock."

Instead of her homework, DJ drew a cartoonish picture of Patches looking forlorn, his eyes more like those of a basset hound than a horse's. The caption inside read, *I'm sorry*. DJ signed it *Love, Patches* and *From me, too. Hope you heal fast. DJ*.

She got the academy roster from her desk drawer and addressed the envelope. She was rummaging in the telephone table for a stamp when the twins hit the door, shouting for her as they advanced. By the time they'd given her the hot fudge sundae they'd brought home, told her all about the school, the clown who made balloon animals, the music, and their teacher, besides the upcoming calendar of events, it was past their bedtime. While Robert and Lindy put them to bed and settled them down, DJ got started on her homework.

Robert and Lindy said good-night to her from the door. "And don't stay up too late," Lindy added. "You look like you need extra sleep, not less."

DJ only nodded. "Night."

They never even asked how my day went.

DJ must have relived the accident fourteen times in her dreams that night. When the alarm buzzed, she felt like she'd just gone to sleep.

She flunked her algebra test.

At the Academy all anyone could talk about was the accident. No one had been seriously hurt on the academy grounds for years. DJ escaped to the horses.

"At least you can't talk about her," she said to Patches as she groomed him for his workout. He snorted and rubbed his forehead against her shoulder, then nosed her pocket for another chunk of carrot.

"Good thing you got hot-walker time, huh?" She patted his neck, already dotted with sweat as he checked out every shadow and movement in the arena. Just jogging him around the oval made her arms tired, the way he pulled at the bit and jigged. Of course, today, every part of her already felt tired. She didn't try to do anything but calm him down for the first half hour until he finally walked flat-footed, jogged, and even loped on an even beat. "I should have kept you out here yesterday to get you over this then."

"No more 'should haves.' " Joe jogged Ranger up beside her.

"Where'd you come from?"

"Oh, I've been here awhile. You were so focused on Patches, you just didn't see me."

"Fine." DJ meant it was anything but. She should have been aware of the entire arena. But she knew better than to say *that* aloud.

"What's up? You look like you lost your last friend."

"I might have. Here Robert has been coaching me and—"

"You're talking about algebra, I take it?"

DJ nodded. "I flunked my algebra test today, and I have to show it to my mother. It'll be a hundred years before I can ride Major again or talk on the phone."

Patches sidestepped and snorted, his ears nearly meeting at the tips.

"Now what?"

The horse backpedaled in hyperspeed. "Come on, Patches, there's nothing there." DJ stopped him and stroked his neck until he calmed down. When he went forward at a walk, she turned again to Joe, who had waited for her.

"On one hand, I hope she sells him and gets a more dependable horse, but on the other hand, I'll really miss this clown. He's going to be a really good horse when he settles down."

"Thanks to you."

"Yeah, right."

After putting Patches up and working with Omega, still on the lunge line but now bridled and under a saddle with the stirrups removed, she took a few minutes with Major. "Joe said he would ride you, but he had to go home to help Gran with the boys." Major nodded and snuffled her cheek. "Sorry I can't take you out." He leaned against her, inviting her to scratch up around his ears. She did so, calling herself all kinds of names at the same time. When she screwed up, she did it big time. If only there was some way to get out of algebra.

"Hey, DJ," Angie called. "Guess what?"

DJ plastered a smile on her face. "What?"

"They got me on some new medicine that is really working. I haven't had an asthma attack for weeks."

"Hey, cool!" DJ gave Major a last pat and left his stall. "The dust from your horse doesn't even bother you?"

Angie shook her head. "Nope. I can breathe."

DJ gave the slender girl a hug. "Now you won't have to miss so many lessons."

"I know. And someday I'll be able to ride like you."

I just hope your mother doesn't ground you from riding like mine does. The thought brought a small spurt of anger.

Krissie and Samantha were tacking up their horses when DJ stopped to talk with them. "Anyone seen Andrew?"

They all shook their heads.

"Did his mom really break her arm in a fall?" Krissie's blue eyes were round.

"She was thrown." Samantha looked to DJ. "Right?"

DJ nodded. "Accidents happen. That's why you have to concentrate on your horse and all that's going on around you at the same time."

"That cat." Sam shook her head, setting her long, thick braid to swinging.

"DJ?"

DJ looked up at the male voice calling her. "Hi, Mr. Johnson. Hi, Andrew." She left the girls and joined the man and his son. "How's your mom, Andrew?"

"Her arm hurts bad."

"It'll get better soon." He wore that shuttered look from back when she began working with him. "Come on, let's get Bandit tacked up. The girls are all ready."

"I've gotta run," Mr. Johnson said. "Have a good class, Andrew. I'll pick you up in . . ." He looked toward DJ.

"Oh, about an hour and a half." She waved back and put an arm about Andrew's shoulders. "You groom Bandit, and I'll help you."

DJ turned to face her waiting students. "You girls go on out to the arena and keep it to a walk until I get there." After the incident the day before, she wasn't taking any chances.

But Andrew's grooming speed would have lost him a snail race.

"Come on, we're late."

"I don't want to." Andrew looked up at her, his brown eyes dressed in fear.

"Once you are mounted, it'll be okay." DJ adjusted the saddle girth.

"No."

DJ stopped and stared at him. *Now what?* She took in a deep breath. "Okay, tell you what we'll do. You stay here with Bandit, and I'll come get you after the girls' lesson. You and I will work together, just us again, okay?"

Andrew stared down at his hands.

"Andrew?"

"Okay."

Even Krissie of the never-ending giggles paid close attention to everything DJ said through the next hour. While DJ missed the banter, she kept a close eye on the girls, the other horse and rider in the arena, and the surrounding area.

"Let's review a bit here," she said, calling them into the center. "What do you do if your horse spooks?"

"Hang on tight!" Krissie clamped her hands around her saddle horn.

"Pull back on the reins and tell your horse to stop," Angie added.

"Keep your legs firm, your rear deep in the saddle, and . . ."

"Don't panic," the three chanted together.

"How can you get your horse to stop running?"

"Pull on the inside rein so he has to go in a tight circle," Sam answered.

"Good. And what's most important?"

"Don't panic!" all three said with wide grins.

"And something else: When your horse has spooked at something, make sure you take him up to it again—lead him if you need to, but show him there is nothing to be afraid of. The sooner you do that, the easier it will be."

"Like getting right back on if you fall off?"

"Exactly." DJ smiled up at them. "You guys are so smart. Now, I've got a new drill for you. Line up down there on the edge of the arena. Then one at a time, I want you to run your horse down to me and pull him to a sliding stop."

"Hey! Way to go!"

One by one, they did so, going from a slow stop to sliding after several run-throughs.

"Good. How did that feel?"

"Fun!"

"More fun when you do it right." Sam rubbed her inner leg where she'd clobbered it against the pommel.

Angie's eyes sparkled. "And the dust didn't even bother me."

"Good. Go ahead and circle the arena at a walk, then head for the barn."

DJ watched them, then held the gate for them to file through. She left them with their mothers and headed to Bandit's stall. She still had to exercise Bunny's horse, too. Maybe she should call and leave a message for her mother that she would be late.

"Andrew?"

Bandit looked up from munching the hay in his manger. His bridle and saddle hung on the stall door. But no Andrew.

17

"HAVE YOU SEEN ANDREW?" DJ asked.

Tony stopped, his horse beside him. "Nope, why?"

"He was supposed to stay with Bandit until I got back. He refused to come to the group class."

"Maybe he went to the bathroom."

"He took the bridle and saddle off Bandit."

"Uh-oh." Tony mounted his horse. "I'll look around outside. Maybe he's waiting for his dad."

DJ asked everyone. Each took off in a different direction, looking, but no one had noticed the boy leaving.

"Where could he go?" DJ asked Bridget back in the office.

"I called his house, but no one answered. I will try again in a minute."

"Maybe someone kidnapped him." Krissie skidded to a stop beside DJ. "We looked everywhere in the barn. Sometimes we hide in the hay bales, but he's not there, either."

"Feed room?" DJ asked.

"Nope, Hilary looked there. We've all looked everywhere."

"Did anyone check the cars and trailers?" Bridget asked.

Amy nodded but grabbed Krissie, calling over her

shoulder. "We'll *really* check them out this time."

"I should have paid more attention to him," DJ moaned. "I told him to wait so I could do a private lesson with him."

"DJ, I do not want to hear 'shoud have' from you again." Bridget grasped DJ's upper arms. "Do you hear me?"

DJ nodded. "But—"

"But nothing. If we do not find him in ten minutes, I will call 9–1–1."

But he was—is—my responsibility. I'm his teacher. His parents trust me to look after him while he's here.

Cries of "Andrew!" echoed from every corner of the academy property, even up by Bridget's house, where no one was allowed to go except with a special invitation.

Could he be hurt somewhere and not able to answer? Is he playing a joke? Where could one small eight-year-old boy go? Or worse, be taken?

The thoughts rampaged through DJ's mind, the last one sending chills up and down her spine—and settling a boulder in her middle. "God, please bring Andrew back. Keep watch over him. Please, God, please." But God hadn't been listening to her prayers lately.

Where did that leave Andrew?

All those at the Academy gathered in the office, shaking their heads and showing empty hands.

"You have looked everywhere?"

They all nodded in reply to Bridget's question.

"In the feed bins?"

"I checked twice," Tony said.

Bridget picked up the phone and dialed the three numbers. "Hello, this is Bridget Sommersby at Briones Riding Academy. I need to report a lost child."

DJ fought the tears gathering at the back of her eyes. Yesterday, Patches spooked and Mrs. Johnson broke her arm. Today, the Johnsons' child was missing. And DJ had been in charge both times. Would the police blame her?

A pin dropping would have sounded like a bowling ball in the room. Someone sniffed.

DJ felt frozen, like she'd been caught playing statue. Only her mind was in motion like a huge flock of blackbirds, all flapping in different directions.

A car drove up and a car door slammed. All eyes turned toward the door. Andrew and his father walked in.

"I found him halfway home. Walking. I hope this hasn't been a problem for you." Mr. Johnson looked around the frozen group.

"Thank you," Bridget told the 9–1–1 dispatcher. "The child and his father just showed up." She put down the phone.

"Uh-oh. I would have called, but my car phone was dead." Mr. Johnson laid a hand on Andrew's shoulder. "I think you owe these people an apology."

"I . . . I'm sorry." New tears joined the tracks already washed on his dusty cheeks.

"I'm sorry, too. I don't know what got into him." Mr. Johnson shook his head. "I thought he was beginning to like riding."

Andrew turned and buried his face in his father's side. Sobs shook his skinny shoulders.

"Aw, that's okay."

"We're just glad you are all right." The academy kids gathered around Andrew.

"Time to get back to work and riding," Bridget announced. "Thank you for all your help and caring."

"Yes, thank you all," Mr. Johnson said, turning to look at everyone. "You're a great bunch of people out here. I'm looking forward to riding myself."

The kids left, many of them giving Andrew a pat on the shoulder as they went by.

DJ crossed the room and knelt in front of the boy. "What is it, Andrew? You've been doing so well."

"H-horses hurt p-people."

Mr. Johnson rolled his eyes. "Andrew, accidents happen. I keep telling you."

DJ thought fast. "Did Bandit hurt you?"

Andrew shook his head.

"Did Patches?"

Another headshake.

"But falling off Patches gave your mother a broken arm?"

Andrew nodded. A huge hiccup shook the boy's body.

"He can't go through life being so scared of everything. That's why we bring him here."

DJ looked up at Mr. Johnson. "He's gotten lots better in the last couple of months. Haven't you, Andrew?"

Andrew let go of this father's jacket and scrubbed his eyes with his fists. He took a deep breath, and when he let it out, his shoulders slumped. "My mother can't ride anymore."

DJ looked at him, trying to figure out where he got that idea. "Only for a while, until her arm heals. Broken bones get better."

"She said Patches is trying to kill her."

"Ah." DJ nodded and looked up at Mr. Johnson.

"Andrew, your mother was joking. She knows Patches didn't do that on purpose. A cat scared him."

"Andrew, what would you do if someone suddenly jumped out and shouted 'boo' at you?"

Andrew looked DJ full in the face. A tear beaded one dark eyelash. "I . . . I'd jump."

"And?" DJ felt like Gran, who had always asked her questions like this.

"Uh . . . ahh . . ."

She waited. Again the room was silent, but this time there were voices coming from outside as the rest of the Academy went about a normal Wednesday afternoon.

"I'd scream."

"Good. Anything else?"

"I . . . I'd run to my mother."

"Or to your bedroom," Mr. Johnson added.

Andrew looked up at him and nodded.

"Okay. The cat scared Patches, right?"

Andrew nodded.

"And Patches wanted to run to his room. Horses always go to their stalls when they are afraid. That's where they feel safe. But something was in his way. What was it?"

"The fence?"

"You got it. Would Patches run into the fence?"

"He could jump over."

"That big fence?"

"Guess not." Andrew shook his head.

"But when he turned fast, your mother didn't turn, too. She fell off."

"And broke her arm." Andrew rubbed his own arm, as if it hurt in sympathy.

"True. But it was an accident." *And riding Patches for her is an accident looking for a chance to happen.*

"Bandit could run away, too."

DJ sighed. This kid knew how to reason. "He could." Thoughts careened around her mind till one stopped for her to catch it. "But Bandit is older and smarter, like your dad here. He doesn't get frightened as easily because he's seen that cat run lots of times. Just like your dad wouldn't jump so easily as you if someone shouted 'boo.' "

Andrew looked up to his father. Mr. Johnson nodded. "DJ is right. I'll come with you so you can ride Bandit now."

Andrew sighed. The kind of sigh that came clear from the soles of his feet. " 'Kay." He took his father's hand. "Will you lead him?"

Mr. Johnson looked at DJ, who nodded back. "I'll get the lunge line for you."

By the time DJ exercised Bunny's horse, Amy had already gone home because she and her mother were going shopping. Joe had left because he and Gran were going into the city to shop.

DJ mounted her bike. The ride home looked to be about a hundred miles—all up hill.

"Your dinner is in the microwave." Lindy turned from helping Bobby and Billy with printing their letters at the dining room table. Her eyes wore that frosty look DJ was coming to recognize—along with the lines in her forehead. Lindy was not pleased with her daughter—again.

"Where's Robert?"

"Working late." This time her mother didn't even look up. "Good one, Billy. Let's try again."

Is she still upset with me from before? DJ didn't know as she trudged up the stairs.

All the way up, one voice in her mind reminded her that if only she hadn't left Andrew alone, this wouldn't have happened. If only she'd been more watchful the day before, she could have chased the cat away before it spooked Patches. If only she'd gotten home on time, her mother might have hugged her.

She snorted at that thought. Her mother didn't like hugging horsey-smelling jerks like her daughter. Who did?

Brad would. And Jackie.

DJ entered her mother's bedroom and picked up the phone. But the answering machine came on with Brad's voice asking the caller to leave a message. DJ set the receiver back in the cradle. They probably went shopping, too. She dialed Joe and Gran's, hoping they had come home. Another message machine.

She could hear her grandmother's voice as if Gran were

right there. *You could talk with God.*

"Yeah, right. He's probably got his answering machine on, too. Maybe He went shopping like everyone else." DJ dragged herself out of her mother's room and back to her own. Rain had been threatening on the way home and now poured down the windows.

She picked up her drawing tablet, then set it down to sharpen her drawing pencils. At least she could do that right. But the horse in the portrait looked more like a mule, and her hand was shaking so badly the lines squiggled.

One of Gran's sayings floated back through her mind. *"When you feel like you're at the end of your rope, pick up your Bible and read until you get a new and stronger hold on that rope."* She always added, *"For that rope is God, and He will never let you go."*

DJ picked up her Bible, and it fell open at the Gospel of John. She started reading the underlined verse: *For God so loved the world . . .* Her eyes blurred until she couldn't see. She flung herself across her bed, the tears soaking the bed-spread.

God, why am I such a flunker? I try and try, and nothing is ever good enough.

Hearing a sound at the door, she pulled the pillow over her head.

"DJ."

"Go away."

She felt her mother sit down on the side of the bed. Her hand felt hot on DJ's jean-covered leg.

"Daddy's home," the boys whispered so loudly it penetrated DJ's fog.

Tears filled her eyes and ears. Sobs tore at her throat, shaking the bed with the force of her cries. The hand stayed on her leg.

"What's wrong?" Robert's voice, quiet and calm.

"DJ's crying awful bad."

"I don't want DJ to cry."

The boys hovered on the verge of crying, she could hear it in their voices. But her own tears wouldn't quit. No matter how hard she tried to choke them back.

She couldn't even quit crying right.

"Darla Jean, what's wrong?" Her mother's voice came soft and gentle, sounding so much like Gran's that DJ cried even harder.

"Come on, boys, it's time for bed." Robert again.

"But DJ won't stop c-crying."

"I love you, DJ. Please." The little-boy voice brought on a new attack.

"You can talk with DJ tomorrow."

"Will she still be crying?" The voices trailed down the hall.

Still her mother sat, stroking her daughter's leg.

Lindy lay down beside DJ, her arm over her daughter's heaving back. "Oh, my dear daughter, if I had only known things were this bad." The stroking continued. "Please forgive me for not paying more attention."

DJ's head pounded. She rubbed her face on the bedspread, trying to wipe away the tears.

"Here." A tissue ended up in DJ's hand. She propped herself on her elbows and blew her nose.

Robert sat down on the other side of her. "You ready to talk now?"

DJ shook her head. "I . . . I just can't d-do anything right."

"Like?"

DJ told them about all the things that were going wrong. About losing Andrew and letting Mrs. Johnson get hurt. About flunking another algebra test, even when Robert helped her. About trying so hard and never catching up. The list continued.

"And us putting more pressure on you?"

Another run of tears. This time DJ was sitting up with both Lindy's and Robert's arms encircling her. More problems flowed out—the noise and bedlam at home all the time, fighting with her mother, the art weekend, giving up Saturdays at the Academy, not riding Major. No time, no time, no time . . .

"I just can't ever do anything good enough." Clutching a clump of tissue, DJ let her hands flop in her lap.

"DJ, if you could quit doing something, what would it be?" Robert laid his hand over hers to stop her from shredding the tissue.

"Algebra."

"Besides that." She could hear a smile in his voice.

DJ thought about all the stuff she'd said. *I don't really want to give up the twins or teaching the girls or* . . . "I guess training Omega because I just started that, and teaching Mrs. Johnson. I'll be done with Bunny's horse by next weekend."

"Why do you take on all that extra work?"

"I need the money. I got behind when I was sick, and spring and summer are the most expensive times of the year with all the shows."

"I see."

DJ sniffed and blew her nose again. She leaned against her mother, grateful for something to prop her up. All her bones felt like pudding. And her muscles drained out with the tears.

"I . . . we . . . ah, DJ wanted a horse and there was no money for that." Lindy blew her own nose. "I guess I thought she would outgrow her 'horse' phase like other girls do."

"No, our DJ has big dreams, and she'll kill herself getting there if we don't help her."

Our DJ. How good that sounded.

"You don't have to help me." DJ tried to straighten up,

but the arms around her didn't let go.

"Ah, but we do. That's what being a family is all about, loving and helping one another." Robert tightened his arm, giving her a hug. "And part of being a family is asking for help. We all get so tied up in what we are doing, we don't always pay close enough attention to *see* when one of the family needs help. Especially when you are so strong and capable and hide your needs."

DJ snorted, then blew her nose again.

"You know, I've never had a teenage daughter before."

"And I've never had twin boys—or a husband." Lindy squeezed this time. "I had you and Gran. We were just starting to work things out on our own when I got married."

"Guess we all have to cut one another some slack, don't you think?"

"Easy for you to say." DJ gave Robert a wobbly smile.

"You're right, DJ—easy to say and hard to do."

DJ's stomach rumbled and grumbled again.

"Did you ever eat?" Lindy asked.

DJ shook her head.

"Me neither, come to think of it." Robert patted his stomach.

"How about we all go raid the kitchen? There must be *something* to eat down there." Lindy got to her feet. "Come on, we can keep talking in the kitchen."

Later, at the table with plates of bacon and eggs before them, Robert said grace. "And please, dear Father, help us all to love one another as you have loved us. Help us to look and listen and ask for help and guidance when we need it. Bless this food and this family. Amen."

DJ's stomach rumbled again.

"I think your stomach is saying amen and let's eat," Robert said with a smile.

"Before the food gets cold." Lindy took a piece of toast from the napkin-lined basket and passed it to DJ.

When they had finished, Robert tented his fingers and tapped them on his chin. "You know, I've been thinking about some of the things you said, DJ."

"Which ones?" she asked before thinking.

"Like about the noise and the boys' loud playing. I think some of that will be taken care of when we move to the new house, and with Maria helping, your mother and I will have more time to be with you kids. We should be able to move out of these close quarters in about two weeks."

"That soon?" Lindy wiped her mouth with her napkin.

"Looks that way."

"Great."

"I've hired a moving company so you won't have to worry about packing. The new furniture won't all be there yet, but we'll have beds and can put this furniture in the family room."

DJ tried to stifle a yawn. She covered her mouth but still nearly cracked her jaw.

"I have a bargain for you."

At the look on his face, she instantly became alert. "What?"

"If you will tell Bridget—or we can tell her if you'd rather—" he took Lindy's hand in his and turned back to DJ—"that you can no longer take on so many responsibilities, then we will gladly pay for any of the things you need beyond what you are able to earn."

DJ looked to her mother.

Lindy nodded. "Money isn't such an issue anymore." She smiled at Robert, then at DJ. "I couldn't pay for anything extra before."

"Now we can."

DJ liked the way he said *we*. "And?"

"And your part of the bargain will be to get and keep your grades up."

DJ groaned. "But even with you coaching me, I flunked the last test."

"So we'll work harder."

There was that *we* word again.

"DJ, all we ask is that you do your best. And that when you need help, you'll ask for it."

"Think of all those people the Olympic winners thank. They each had help and plenty of it to get where they are." Lindy reached for DJ's hand. "And they always start with their family."

DJ thought of the twins asleep upstairs. She looked at the man and woman across the table from her. She had Gran and GJ, too, plus Brad and Jackie, and aunts and uncles and cousins. Friends like Amy, and Bridget for a coach. And God, too. He had to be working in all this.

"I'll have a big list to thank, too. And I won't *try* to do my best. I *will* do my best."

"Thata girl." Robert held out his hand and shook hers. "I have a favor to ask."

DJ looked at him, *now whats* running through her brain.

"To keep your mother and Gran happy, if I pay your way to the jumping clinic Gray is teaching over in Sacramento, will you please go to the art workshop?"

"You mean I could do both?"

"Joe says he'll go along, too."

"When is the one in Sacramento?"

"The following weekend. You have nothing else going on—I checked." Robert leaned forward.

DJ looked at him. "You really mean I can do both?"

"Yes."

"Then of course I will. I'm not a total idiot, just stubborn."

"That's the understatement of the year. You, my dear daughter, wrote the book on being stubborn. But the other side of being stubborn or bullheaded—" Lindy paused—"is perseverance. And that's a mighty fine trait to have."

"Just like a couple of others I know in this family?" Robert asked, rising to his feet. He picked up his dishes and motioned for the others to do the same. "Like you, Lindy, getting your masters in spite of a full-time job and a family, and Gran becoming a nationally known illustrator."

"Hey, how come you're so smart about all this family business?" Lindy asked.

"I talked to Pastor Dave at my church in San Francisco, read a couple of books on blended families, and wore my knees down praying. I want us to be the kind of family God talks about in the Bible. I want us to be open and honest and loving."

"And close?" DJ asked.

"Even in close quarters." Robert flung an arm over her shoulders. "*Especially* in close quarters."

The three of them walked under the arch into the family room, arm in arm.

Coming Fall 1998!

Will moving day ever come? One delay after another prohibits DJ and her family from moving into their new house. Tension is thick and tempers flare—all DJ wants is some *space* to herself. But when the time finally arrives, DJ realizes she's about to leave the only home she's ever known. And she isn't sure she's ready to say good-bye. Is DJ prepared for what lies ahead? Don't miss Book #7 in the HIGH HURDLES series!

Teen Series From
Bethany House Publishers

Early Teen Fiction (11–14)

THE ALLISON CHRONICLES by Melody Carlson
Follow along as Allison O'Brian, the daughter of a famous 1940s movie star, searches for the truth about her past and the love of a family.

HIGH HURDLES by Lauraine Snelling
Show jumper DJ Randall strives to defy the odds and achieve her dream of winning Olympic Gold.

SUMMERHILL SECRETS by Beverly Lewis
Fun-loving Merry Hanson encounters mystery and excitement in Pennsylvania's Amish country.

THE TIME NAVIGATORS by Gilbert Morris
Travel back in time with Danny and Dixie as they explore unforgettable moments in history.

Young Adult Fiction (12 and up)

CEDAR RIVER DAYDREAMS by Judy Baer
Experience the challenges and excitement of high school life with Lexi Leighton and her friends.

GOLDEN FILLY SERIES by Lauraine Snelling
Tricia Evanston races to become the first female jockey to win the sought-after Triple Crown.

JENNIE MCGRADY MYSTERIES by Patricia Rushford
A contemporary Nancy Drew, Jennie McGrady's sleuthing talents bring back readers again and again.

LIVE! FROM BRENTWOOD HIGH by Judy Baer
The staff of an action-packed teen-run news show explores the love, laughter, and tears of high school life.

THE SPECTRUM CHRONICLES by Thomas Locke
Adventure and romance await readers in this fantasy series set in another place and time.

SPRINGSONG BOOKS by various authors
Compelling love stories and contemporary themes promise to capture the hearts of readers.

WHITE DOVE ROMANCES by Yvonne Lehman
Romance, suspense, and fast-paced action for teens committed to finding pure love.

9712